JUST LIKE THE MOVIES

The if  line

JUST LIKE THE MOVIES

An IF ONLY *novel*

Kelly Fiore

BLOOMSBURY

NEW YORK LONDON OXFORD NEW DELHI SYDNEY

First published in the United States of America in July 2014
by Bloomsbury Children's Books
Paperback edition published in February 2016
www.bloomsbury.com

Bloomsbury is a registered trademark of Bloomsbury Publishing Plc

For information about permission to reproduce selections from this book, write to
Permissions, Bloomsbury Children's Books, 1385 Broadway, New York, New York 10018
Bloomsbury books may be purchased for business or promotional use. For information on
bulk purchases please contact Macmillan Corporate and Premium Sales Department at
specialmarkets@macmillan.com

The Library of Congress has cataloged the hardcover edition as follows:
Fiore, Kelly.
Just like the movies / Kelly Fiore.
pages   cm
Summary: Pretty, popular Marijke Monti and overachieving nerd-girl Lily Spencer have little in
common—except that neither feels successful when it comes to love. Now they have a budding
friendship and a plan—to act out grand gestures and get the guys of their dreams.
ISBN 978-1-61963-354-4 (hardcover) • ISBN 978-1-61963-355-1 (e-book)
[1. Love—Fiction. 2. Friendship—Fiction.] I. Title.
PZ7.F49869Jus 2014   [Fic]—dc23   2013046922

ISBN 978-1-61963-356-8 (paperback)

Book design by Amanda Bartlett
Typeset by Westchester Book Composition
Printed and bound in USA by Berryville Graphics, Berryville, Virginia
2 4 6 8 10 9 7 5 3 1

All papers used by Bloomsbury Publishing, Inc., are natural, recyclable products
made from wood grown in well-managed forests. The manufacturing processes
conform to the environmental regulations of the country of origin.

For Lily and Eila,
who are brave, smart,
beautiful, talented,
fearless, and real.
And, most of all, who are loved.

JUST LIKE THE MOVIES

⤐ COMING ATTRACTIONS ⤐

The music practically floats out of the speakers; it fills up the fenced yard, flies over the swing set, and spins into eddies under the deck. Peter Gabriel's voice is gruff and soft in all the best ways, but my arms are already tired and I've been holding this speaker dock over my head for less than a minute. How did John Cusack do it with a boom box three times this size?

Behind me, Lily shifts in the overgrowth at the edge of the Lawsons' property. The spotlight she's holding stutters, then points up at the trees. I turn to glare back at her just as she fixes her aim. I'm immediately blinded by the beam of light.

"Sorry," she says in a stage whisper. I shake my head and turn to face the house. Peter's just reached the chorus, but there's still no sign of Tommy.

I'm starting to second-guess this approach. *Say Anything* is a classic movie, but I have no idea if Tommy will get the reference or if he'll understand how devoted the main character, Lloyd, was to his true love, Diane. If he'll know that the words of this song say everything I'm feeling about him. If he'll realize that it says everything I want him to feel about me.

No lights in the windows, no doors opening. I glance back at Lily, who shrugs.

"Maybe no one's home," she suggests. I shake my head.

"They're home. Maybe it isn't loud enough . . ."

I lower my arms and practically groan with the relief of a renewed blood supply, then switch the volume up five more notches. I take a deep breath and raise the speaker dock back up over my head. It's hard to remember why we thought this was a good idea, now that I can't feel my fingers.

And then a light goes on in one of the bedroom windows, shining a hazy golden glow over the yard. I suck in a breath and push the speakers even higher, as though that will make all the difference.

The light doesn't go off, but no one comes to the window and no other lights turn on. I squint up at the second floor, trying to calculate which bedroom it's from. Tommy's house is so big that it's really hard to figure out, especially since his room is in the middle of half a dozen others. I bite my lip. I really hope I didn't wake his snotty sister, Gina, who's home from college this weekend. The last thing I need is to explain myself to Tommy's family.

"Marijke? Is that you?"

A man's voice calls out from the darkness. A man's voice that isn't Tommy's.

The back door is open now and there are footsteps on the deck stairs. I peer at the pale-blue-robed figure moving toward me. Behind him, another one follows. Unsure of my next move, I lower my arms and press pause on the iPod. The immediate silence is unsettling, and I can suddenly hear my racing heartbeat.

Tommy's parents are standing ten feet away from me. I swallow. They don't look mad, exactly. But they don't look happy either. How am I supposed to explain this to them? At least, how can I explain it in a way that doesn't sound completely insane? I consider my options.

I want your son to love me, so I'm acting out movie scenes.

Say Anything *is just the beginning. There are a dozen others I'm willing to try.*

Haven't you ever wished you could fall in love like they do on-screen?

I set down the speakers. This is something Lily and I didn't plan for. It's ten at night and I'm standing in front of my boyfriend's parents. If this were a movie, the director would call "Cut!" But this is real life, not a movie set, and there isn't a script to follow.

PART ONE

THE FOLLOWING PREVIEW HAS BEEN
APPROVED FOR ALL AUDIENCES

ONE

⟹ MARIJKE ⟸

There's something you should know about me: I've spent my whole life leaping tall buildings in a single bound.

Well, replace *leaping* with *hurdling*.

And replace *tall buildings* with *hurdles*.

And replace *my whole life* with *the last three years*.

Still, I feel like Superman—or Super*wo*man—standing here at the starting line. This is it—this race is the one that will or will not qualify me for the Virginia State Track and Field Competition, or "states" as it's called by most of my teammates. I'm lucky that the county track meet is at Molesworth High School, my home school, because I know this track better than I know a lot of my friends. I certainly spend more time with it lately than I do with them.

As a rule I don't really get nervous, but clearly my opponent does. She's pouring sweat like there's a prize for

Heaviest Perspirer. I turn to face the track and gaze out at the hurdles. The first one is fifteen yards from my feet, this line, and the sweat-soaked girl next to me. It's nothing new or different, but the distance is always worth acknowledging. Just like how I have to greet each of the hurdles. Since you have to shake hands with your human rival, I figure you should recognize your real opponents on the track. In high school, there are eight hurdles over the course of three hundred meters. An hour before every meet, I walk the whole track and give a little nod to each and every hurdle. Once they've been acknowledged, they can be dismissed.

I'm a sprint hurdler. To me, the distance races are sort of a yawn. It's like the difference between taking a shortcut versus the scenic route, and when the destination is states, I'd like to get there as quickly as possible. But first I've got to wait for the jumpers to get their highs and longs on. Once they finish leaping over their tall buildings, I can get back to mine.

I look over at the bleachers on the sidelines. My parents are sitting on their favorite bench in the third row. Dad says it has the best angle for the video camera, which is currently trained on me. When Mom sees me, she elbows him, points at me, and they both wave manically. They're wearing matching Molesworth polo shirts, and my mom has spirit ribbons woven through her blond braid. Even from here, I can tell that they're holding hands. My parents have been together since they met here at Molesworth High almost twenty years ago. It's the kind of love story you've seen in a dozen romantic comedies—Mom was head cheerleader, Dad was the quarterback of the football team, they were king and queen of their junior and senior proms, and they were voted Cutest Couple in the yearbook.

On all sides of my parents are cheering, excited fans. It's hard to believe how many people actually came out for the meet today. Girls' track has become such a big deal at Molesworth that the varsity cheerleaders were recruited from boys' basketball to give us some encouragement. I glance over at the long line of girls decked out in black and gold-that-isn't-really-gold-but-actually-just-dark-yellow and notice a streak of blue breaking up the school-spirit rainbow. My boyfriend, Tommy Lawson, lead guitarist of our school's hottest jam band, has stolen a set of pom-poms from one of the sophomores. The sparkly accessories clash with his vintage Aerosmith T-shirt and ripped jeans. The girl—Jenny? Mary?—giggles and swats at him as he pretends to do a cheer. He just grins at her and dashes down the line, bopping each girl on the head with a pom-pom along the way. All the girls—and I mean *all* the girls—turn to give Tommy a smile or a wink or a flirty little wave. This is what I get for dating one of the hottest guys in school. The competition is fierce—and it's wearing spandex and eyeliner.

I bite down hard on the inside of my cheek and bend down to tighten my laces. I need to stay focused on my body and this race, not on Tommy's habit of flirting with every girl within a five-foot radius. I re-pony my ponytail, making sure each blond strand is tucked into my hair elastic. As I start stretching my hamstrings for the umpteenth time, I see Coach Mason crossing the field. When he gets closer, he gives me a double thumbs-up.

"You got this, Marijke. You know you do," he calls out.

I agree. I know I do. But I just smile.

Then Coach gives me his trademark "air high five." He's really afraid of touching students, even via the high five, which is possibly the lamest of all physical contact. We slap air, keeping our hands a foot apart, before he hurries off the track toward the sidelines.

Just then, there's a fuzzy crackle over the loudspeaker and the announcer calls for hurdlers to move to their lanes. Sweaty McSweaterson and I take our marks and get into position. I focus on the track in front of me and force myself to concentrate. I'm not thinking about my opponent shaking off like a wet dog, perspiration flying in all directions. I'm not thinking about the pressure to win, which has weighed heavy on my shoulders like a chain-link blanket for the past several weeks. And I'm certainly, absolutely *not* thinking about my boyfriend flirting with cheerleaders while I prepare to compete in the biggest race of my life.

The shotgun fires and I almost hesitate. Almost, but not quite.

There are two Marijkes right now—the one who is back at the starting line worrying about Tommy, and the one who is already past the first low hurdle. As I fly over one after the other, I forget everything.

This is the only time I'm ever really alone—out here, running, racing with nothing but my body to answer to.

I'm not a part of a couple or a family or a team.

I'm just me.

As my feet hit the pavement, it's almost a rhythm. All my senses are on high alert. I can feel my opponent's footfalls next to me, vibrating the track. I can smell the freshly cut grass as I inhale through my nose and exhale from my mouth. My body knows how to do this. It gets its butt into gear and it drives me forward toward my goal. This is the time when I'm most relaxed, which is sort of ironic, since every part of me is taking action. Still, I feel at home in this moment. And it always passes me by way too fast.

I'm past the last white line before I even recognize what it is. By the time I've stopped, I'm a dozen yards past the finish. Coach is screaming his head off and my team is swarming onto the field and racing toward me. For a second, I think I've done something wrong.

Then I realize that I've won—that *we've* won. Molesworth girls' track is going to states.

"That wasn't even close!" Beth, our team captain, is breathless and gleeful. "Your competition's stutter step threw her off before she even got to the first hurdle. Girl didn't have a chance against you!"

I feel a little bad when I see my sopping-wet opponent, who seems to be dripping tears this time instead of sweat. But as my team raises me up onto Beth's shoulders, I can't help but feel thrilled. We've worked so hard for this. *I've* worked so hard for this. It's the spring semester of my senior year and finally, FINALLY, we're going to states.

I shield my eyes and see my parents hopping around on the outskirts of the crowd, spraying Silly String at each other. I shake my head, smiling despite myself. Mom and Dad lack that chip in their brains that tells them certain behavior isn't normal for adults. They have water-balloon fights. They order kids' meals at restaurants. All the high scores on the Wii are theirs. On more than one occasion I've caught them half-dressed, making out on the couch.

So. Gross.

Still, when Beth finally sets me down, I hurry through the throng of well-wishers to hug them.

"You go, girlfriend!" my dad calls out. "Rock on with your bad self!"

I roll my eyes. "Dad, your attempt at teen slang is so totally out of date."

"Don't be hatin'!" he says. I look over at Mom, but she just grins back at me.

"Have you guys seen Tommy?" I ask, craning my neck to look over the crowd.

"Oh, he's around here somewhere," my mom says, clinging to my arm. "Honey, we're just so proud of you!"

I let them shower me with compliments for a few more minutes until I see Tommy at the opposite end of the bleachers. I pry myself loose from my mother's grasp.

"Tommy!" I call out, breaking into a jog. My legs ache in protest, but I ignore their complaints.

Tommy turns around with that sexy smile only he can give—all lips, totally luscious. His dark hair is rumpled and he's got that five-o'clock shadow that makes him look more like a man than a boy. I love the way his blue eyes crinkle up at the corners when he sees me. It's like I'm the only girl in the world when he looks at me like that.

And then I notice the three girls sitting on the other side of him.

"Hey." I reach out and grab his hand. He doesn't seem to mind as he pulls me into him. "Hey Jenny. Millie. Nina." I nod at each girl and think of the hurdles. Acknowledge and dismiss.

"Hey Marijke," Millie drawls, a sugary smile spreading across her bronzed face. "Congrats on the win."

"Thanks." I snake my left arm around Tommy's waist, then tilt my head up and smile at him.

"Thanks for coming."

"Anything for you." He leans down to kiss me, and it

feels as good as always—wet and miraculous and oh-so-hot. I can't help but bat my eyelashes at him. When I'm around Tommy, I always feel totally love-struck. Sometimes when I look at him, it's hard to believe that we've been together over a year now.

"Well, we'll let you two celebrate," Millie says. All three girls stand and smooth down their too-short skirts.

"Bye Tommy," Nina says, giving a wiggly finger wave that makes me want to break her hand.

"How about you get your own, Nina?" I mutter under my breath as she heads down the bleachers behind her friends. She doesn't hear me, but Tommy does; he elbows my side lightly.

"Be nice."

"Why should I? She clearly wants you."

Tommy laughs and gives my shoulders a squeeze.

"You, my love, are just jealous."

"Maybe," I grumble.

There's that word: "love." I wish it didn't affect me so much when Tommy says it, but it does—mostly because he says it a lot, but never with "I" before it and "you" after it. There's lots of love in our relationship. There are e-mails and texts signed with "love." But no actual "I love you." Not yet.

"So, how does it feel to be a state champ?" he's asking me. I smile and shake my head.

"County. *County* champ. States are two weeks away in Salverton."

"Right, right. So, how does it feel to be a *county* champ?" he amends, tugging my ponytail. He places a hand at the small of my back, and I start feeling that warm, gushy sensation invade my belly.

"You know what?" I say, grinning. "It feels pretty darn good."

High above our heads, the loudspeaker crackles to life. I squint up at the press box, where our new athletic director, Mr. Saunders, is standing at the microphone.

"Marge-uh-kuh? Marge-uh-kuh Monti?"

"It's MA-RAY-KUH!" I yell up to him. "And that's me."

"Well, Ma-ray-kuh," he says slowly, emphasizing every syllable, "a young man offered to clean the boys' locker room for a month if I played this song for you."

The speakers buzz and I glance around, confused, as the music starts. It takes me a minute to hear the low, husky voice through the static; when I finally do, I'm totally shocked. I turn to face Tommy.

"That's you singing?"

"Yup."

"You had them play a song for me?"

"Yup."

I throw my arms around his neck. "I can't believe you! This might be the sweetest thing you've ever done!"

He sweeps me into his arms and pulls off an improvised, if sloppy, waltz to his band's song "Blue Morning." It's times like this when I know that my obsession with three little words is just silly. It's obvious that Tommy loves me. I mean, he wouldn't have done something this romantic if he didn't, right?

TWO

I don't know what I was thinking when I said I could come to school on a Saturday. I am *such* a sucker.

Spread out in front of me are two county maps, a list of bus drivers as long as my arm, and at least six hundred children's books. When I told the Student Government Association I'd spearhead our MobileStories Bookmobile initiative, I didn't think that would translate to mapping routes, organizing drivers, and boxing books by myself over the weekend.

"This is what I get for volunteering," I say aloud to the empty room. "It's not Meagan or Courtney who are sacrificing their cheerleading engagements for the sake of a good cause."

I look up at the wall clock. I've been here for more than four hours now and I'm still not done. My mom always says I need to learn to rely on other people for help. I'd say she's right if there *were* any other people to rely on around here.

"SGA secretary doesn't equal whipping boy, Lily," she'd said this morning as I poured myself a second mug of coffee.

"It does when you're trying for a full ride to Virginia University."

Mom sighed. "You've been accepted—that's the first step."

"It will look good on internship applications," I said between sips of my favorite French roast. "And my résumé. And . . . you know . . . other stuff with lists."

"Right. Because you need *more* volunteer work on your applications and your résumé. You might be the only student in history to have a separate page attached just for your philanthropy."

"And *you* might be the only parent in the world who discourages her daughter from giving back."

Mom shook her head. "I'm not saying you shouldn't give back, honey. I'm just saying that you already give so much—I can't help but worry that there won't be anything left for you."

"Yeah, I feel the same way about some of the dates you've been on lately," I muttered under my breath.

Now, though, I'm still thinking about her words as I run my rainbow of highlighters over the three different bookmobile routes. It's not like I'm *always* the one in charge. When it comes to the dances and the pep rallies—well, I leave those kinds of hype jobs to my peppier counterparts, SGA president, Courtney, and her VP, Meagan.

Let's be honest, if we're trying for sheer numbers of people or quantity of enthusiasm, I'm not the best representative of our senior class. Last week, two girls in gym asked me if I was a new student. When I reminded them that we'd had math together—in middle school—they looked at me suspiciously, like I was making the whole thing up. The only reason I even got to be SGA secretary was that there was a last-minute opening and no time for new elections. The principal just pulled my name from a list of students with high GPAs and no discipline record. What's worse than being excluded? Being included by default, courtesy of school administration. There's nothing like a principal's endorsement to solidify one's unpopularity.

There are some advantages to flying under the radar like I do. By working behind the scenes, I never get a lot of credit, but I also don't have to field the blame. When people hated last year's Honky-Tonk Hoedown theme for the fall dance, I didn't have to answer for it. When Vegateens, the vegan students' association, complained about the portrayal of poultry in our "Don't Chicken Out—Come to the Student-Teacher Basketball Game" slogan, I let Courtney handle the fallout.

Of course, sometimes it would be nice to get a *little* credit. It's kind of weird to be such a big part of things but not a part of things at all. At least not enough to be recognized. Most of the time, I just try to convince myself that I don't care.

I pull myself up to standing and stretch my legs. A tangle of black curls flops over my forehead and I repin it with a clip; the unruliness of my hair always feels a little ironic, considering how quiet I am and how unrestrained my curls are. They demand attention. I demand bobby pins.

I'm about to start boxing up the last of the books when, through the half-open window, I hear the roar of a cheering crowd. I'd almost forgotten that the county track meet was today; it was part of the reason I'd been saddled with this big job by myself. Courtney, Meagan, and the rest of the cheerleaders had to be there, but most of the student government representatives wanted to go too. As for me, I could count on one hand the number of sporting events I'd been to in high school.

Or, you know, *ever.*

The cheering continues, and I move to the window to squint out toward the lower sports fields. From here, the trees block most of the track and what I can see is fuzzy. I'm sure I'll know soon enough if the Molesworth High girls' track team made it to states. Then there will be more pep rallies and posters and fund-raisers for spirit T-shirts.

With every winning moment comes more work and more planning.

"Lily?"

Mrs. Thatcher is standing in the doorway of the Student Activity office. She's got her arms crossed and eyebrows raised in a way that makes me want to apologize for being here.

"I've got permission," I say. She shakes her head.

"I have no doubt you do. I was just wondering why you are up here by yourself when you could be down at the track with your classmates, celebrating our victory."

You know, it really solidifies my lameness that I learn about the big school news from my history teacher instead of a fellow student. I force a smile and move back to my boxes of books.

"I'm almost done here." I look around at the floor, still covered with picture books. "Well, as done as I'm going to get today."

"Don't tell me you're coming back tomorrow. It's Sunday!"

I shrug noncommittally. Mrs. Thatcher smiles.

"Well, no one could accuse you of not being dedicated," she says as she walks back toward her classroom.

I almost snort. No one would ever accuse me of anything. They'd have to remember my name first.

The celebrations outside have died down when I lock up

the SA office and head out the school's main entrance. The parking lot is almost empty but covered in ribbon and confetti. When I reach my Corolla, I untangle a long black streamer from the antenna.

Great. My *car* was a bigger part of the festivities than I was.

I could go straight home, leaving MHS and my long to-do list behind me. But I can't help myself. I feel the lick of anticipation over my skin as I drive along the side of the school. I pull into the gravel auxiliary lot, then slow the car down to a crawl and look out at the motocross track below.

Through the haze of brown dust, I can see at least half a dozen motorcycles on the course. The league is only two years old, but it hasn't had any trouble attracting participants. When the idea came up to start a high school motocross team, the school board balked. A few other schools in the area were piloting programs, but they weren't without risks. But Joe Lombardi, the current team captain, was really convincing.

Of course, it helped that his uncle was Bobby Lombardi, X Games Rallycross competitor, who was willing to fund the entire operation.

I can see Joe now, standing at the sidelines with his arms crossed over his chest and his helmet grasped in one hand. Even from here he looks focused. I bet his dark hair is a little damp from sweat, and I picture his eyebrows, knitted together, as he strategizes the jumps and turns of the track. I can practically see him biting his full bottom lip and squinting his sexy green eyes at the racers around him, his gaze intense and calculating and confident.

So yeah, I have a huge, crazy crush on Joe Lombardi.

And he doesn't know I exist.

I sigh and turn away, punching the gas so the gravel spits out from under my tires.

Let's face it—it's about as much of a daredevil as I'll ever be.

THREE

⇒ MARIJKE ⇐

There is nothing, *nothing* in the world that feels better than being in Tommy's arms. Especially when he's done something like *this*—played a song just for *me* in front of all these people. I can see the faces of the cheerleading squad and even some of my track teammates—they're totally wishing they were me right now. I can't blame them. I'd be jealous of me too.

"And if you liked that, folks," Mr. Saunders is half-shouting over the loudspeaker, "Tommy Lawson and his band will be playing at Skinners tonight at 8 p.m.!"

A couple of the cheerleaders give a little squeal.

"You guys are playing at Skinners?" one of them says. "That is so *hot*!"

I pull back to look at Tommy, surprised.

"You're playing tonight?"

"Yeah. Sorry, baby." He cups my chin. "It was a last-minute gig. You understand, right?"

I look down at my hands. Yeah, I understand.

I understand that Tommy loves his music and is serious about his band.

I understand that there are a gazillion girls who would kill for a date with my hot boyfriend.

And I understand *no one* likes a nag or a clinger as a girlfriend.

So I just nod, even though there is only one thing I actually understand—that I just won the county track meet and I want to celebrate with Tommy and my teammates.

"Pizza?" he asks, his hand still on my face. I force a brilliant smile.

"Please. I'm starving."

"Want to go tell your parents where you're going?"

I shake my head. "They know I'm riding over with you. The pizza pig-out is a post-run ritual."

He heads up to the parking lot while I grab my gear and work my way back to the locker room. The team's high spirits have been replaced by hunger. After every meet we head over to Salvatore's Pizza Bar. Some people consider going there a good-luck charm, but I think we go because there's a $5.99 all-you-can-eat special. Put twenty-five runners in a room with unlimited pizza and you'll see what speed and focus *really* is.

A few minutes later, I'm standing in the parking lot, freshly showered and peering out at the line of cars idling along the sidewalk. Tommy beeps the horn of his 1969 Dodge Charger, and I grin as I reach the car and slide into the passenger seat.

"Hey, General Qi," I say to the car, patting the dash. It's the same model as the *Dukes of Hazzard* General Lee, so Tommy named it General Qi to "harness its energy." I don't think it's working, since it still breaks down an awful lot.

"You hungry?" I ask Tommy as he swings the car out onto the main road. He shrugs.

"A little. I'm more stressed about playing tonight."

Then don't play, I think.

"Don't be," I say. "You guys are getting really good."

Tommy looks over at me. "*Getting* good? We aren't good yet?"

Ugh. I shouldn't have said anything.

One of the best and worst of Tommy's traits is his sensitivity. It means that he loves puppies and sad movies and he still sleeps with a stuffed moose. It also means that he gets really defensive, especially when I say something about his music.

"No, of course not. You *are* good." I try to backpedal. "It's just an expression."

"Right. I guess it's hard to impress *you* since you're such a rock star on the track. My *little band* just can't compete."

"That's not what I even—"

"Whatever. Just forget it."

I look out the window. I've learned that now is *not* the time to try to convince him that I just want to be helpful. Right now he just wants to pout.

Even though Tommy is, like, überconfident, he feels like he should be getting noticed for his music as much as I'm getting noticed for my running. His band has been together for a year now and they practice four days a week, at least. He's said to me multiple times that he doesn't understand why they haven't gotten their "big break" yet. The thing is . . . well, they're a *high school* band. I would never say it to him, but I'm not sure how successful high school bands can even be, unless they have an arrangement with Disney or their name rhymes with "Dustin Dieber."

We're both silent for the rest of the drive, but when we pull into the Salvatore's parking lot, Tommy's clearly decided to let it go. He shifts the car into park, then leans over and gives me a kiss.

"Congratulations again, baby."

"Thank you," I say, still a bit put out. His hand travels up and down my bare arm. The goose bumps are immediate, and he gives me that look—the one that tempts me into going further and further with him every time we make out. I press a finger to his lips and I can't help but smile.

"I need to feed my *stomach* hunger first," I say. He sighs.

"Yeah, okay." He fiddles with his keys, still in the ignition, then turns back to look at me. "Listen, I think I'm gonna jet."

"What?" I blink. "But what about getting pizza?"

Tommy runs a hand through his hair. "I just want to go jam for a while. I told the guys we'd go through the set before we play tonight."

"Oh. Okay." I don't even bother trying to hide my disappointment.

"Don't say it like that."

He's giving me the puppy-dog, lip-quivering, don't-send-me-to-the-doghouse look. Again I try not to smile, but when it comes to Tommy, my lips are total traitors.

"There's the smile I love," he says, and he almost sounds triumphant. Like he's won something.

"You'll catch a ride with one of the girls?" he's asking, already shifting the car into reverse. I nod.

"Sure. Good luck tonight."

"You're sure you can't come?"

I laugh, but it's hard and brittle. "To Skinners? No dice. My parents are cool, but they're never going to let me go to a biker bar."

"It's a pool hall, Marijke."

"Yeah. With an eighteen-or-older policy."

Tommy nods. "You know, we really should work on getting you a fake ID."

"I'll be eighteen in six months."

"So? Wouldn't it be fun to have an extra half a year of fake legality?"

I shrug.

"I think half the senior class is gonna be there tonight," Tommy muses. I wait for the "but I wish you were coming too." It never happens.

Instead, I open the passenger door. "Well, have fun."

And I think, *I love you.*

But I say, "I'll miss you."

Tommy winks. "Right back atcha, baby."

And then he's gone. Reverse, neutral, drive, and Tommy has sped off into the dusk like something that was meant to disappear. Sometimes Tommy just isn't sensitive to my feelings, despite the fact that he's such an emotionally open guy. Sometimes he upsets me when he doesn't mean to. And on nights like tonight, I feel like everything is a competition. Who can win Tommy's attention? Who can be his top priority?

"Marijke!"

There's a chorus of female voices behind me, and I turn to see some of the track team hanging out of the glass door, motioning for me to come in.

I smile at them and shake my head to clear it. I'm going to go in there, I'm going to have a good time, and I'm going to remember why I'm here tonight—to celebrate my team, how far we've made it, and what I've actually won.

FOUR

 LILY

By the time I pull into the driveway of our three-bedroom rancher, I've managed to banish Joe back to the "never going to happen" realm of my brain.

Instead, I'm mentally ticking the boxes of what I need to do tonight: I've got a lab report to finish, a scholarship essay to write, and a list of bookmobile drivers to call. Not to mention that I may or may not be cooking dinner for my little brother, Mac. I can't remember if tonight is a date night or not.

But then again, most nights are when it comes to my mom.

My mother is in love with love. She desperately wants the lead role in a real-life romantic comedy. Granted, her life hasn't been all flowers and chocolates. She had me at seventeen but still managed to graduate high school and get her dental hygienist license from the local community college. I was seven when she met Mac's father, eight when they married, nine when Mac was born, and ten when his father left. Four years is the longest any guy has stuck around. Let's be honest—with two kids, Mom's pickings have started getting slim.

But really, another father figure is the last thing our family needs. Not that it matters. When it comes to love, Mom doesn't seem to have a head on her shoulders. She's all heart.

And that means it gets broken. A lot.

I come in through the garage and hang my jacket in the mud room, then pick up Mac's dirty cleats and toss them out the door.

"I told him to do that an hour ago," Mom calls from the kitchen. I peek around the corner and see her at the stove. She smiles and waves an oven mitt as I drop my books on the kitchen table.

"You're home tonight?" I ask, surprised. She shakes her head.

"Not for long. I just wanted to get some pasta boiling for you and Mac."

Then I realize that she's in full date makeup—fake eyelashes and all—and that her hair is in rollers. I take the wooden spoon from her hand and wave her away from the stove.

"I'll do this. Go finish getting"—I look at her short skirt and tight tank top—"ready."

"Thanks, babe." She kisses my cheek, and I smell the cotton candy lip gloss that makes me gag. I don't know why she insists on wearing something marketed specifically for twelve-year-old girls.

"Who is it this time?" I ask as she heads for the door.

"Jim."

"Oh, right. Jim." I have no idea who Jim is.

"You remember." Mom is looking at me, a little impatient. "The contractor? The one who was remodeling Dr. Benson's kitchen?"

"Oh, *that* Jim," I say sarcastically. "Sure, Mom. I *totally* remember him."

Dr. Benson is Mom's boss. His house is both his office, in the front, and his residence, in the back. I bet it's nice to roll out of bed and walk into work, but I'm sure it gets old sharing your house with patients, employees, and, apparently, a contractor named Jim.

"Yeah, so," Mom is saying, her voice a little breathy with excitement, "I think he's taking me to Skinners to see some band, so that should be fun."

I just nod. I don't know what Skinners is. I don't *want* to know what Skinners is. I mean, I know what Skinners sounds like and that alone makes me want to hurl.

"But I shouldn't be home too late," she adds as she walks out the door.

"Famous last words," I snort.

When kind-of-bald-and-sort-of-chubby Jim picks up my mom, he makes a good show of shaking my hand and kneeling down to Mac's level. He asks me about school and then promptly ignores my answer, while watching my mom adjust her cleavage in the hall mirror. He ruffles Mac's hair as they leave. When the door shuts, Mac just looks at me.

"Does he think I'm the family dog?"

I shrug. "Maybe." Then I sling an arm around his shoulder. "Mom made some pasta, but I'm thinking pizza. What do you say?"

"I say yes!"

Thirty minutes later, Mac and I are pigging out on pepperoni thin crust and watching repeats of *Ice Road Truckers* until he gets distracted by the lure of his Nintendo DS. I pull my scholarship essay up on the family laptop, but as I stare at the screen, the little blinking cursor taunts me.

Write something brilliant, it says. *There are a million girls just like you—great grades, long résumés—and they have actual activities on their list of accolades. You know, like student athletes. Prom queens. Class presidents. Girls who are a* part *of life, not just living on the edge of it.*

Clearly I have a very judgmental cursor.

I start typing my answer to "Describe how your high school experience has impacted your desire to pursue higher education," but all my answers are coming out monosyllabic and shallow.

My high school life was good.

It taught me things.

I like things.

Things are good.

I close the laptop.

Resigned, I grab the remote and flop back on the couch, flipping through the first few hundred channels. The next time I glance at the clock, it's a little before ten and I remember Mom's promise of coming home at a reasonable time. If she actually meant it, I've still got a few good hours before she'll pour herself into bed.

"Mac," I yell, then listen for my brother's voice. In the distance, I can hear some electronic combat sounds. It's like a cat with a bell, except the bell has automatic weapons and lots of ammunition.

"Mac!" I try again.

"Yeah?"

"Bed soon, buddy."

He hesitates. "Just another ten minutes. I linked the DS with Nathan and Geoff. We're trying to kill off the world-dominating aliens."

"Oh, well, carry on then. Thanks for preserving our freedom."

Sometimes I'm jealous that Mac has good friends, but

most of the time I'm glad. I never really managed to make the connection with anyone the way he has. Of course, we moved around a lot more when I was his age. By the time we settled here, it was as though I'd missed out on picking teams. The friends and groups were already decided, so I just kind of wove around the cliques, hoping I'd absorb like in cell osmosis. I didn't. Like all inhospitable hosts, they rejected the unfamiliar. I have people I'm friendly with but not actual friends—not the way other people do, at least.

I flip through a few more channels until *Pitch Perfect* pops up on HBO. It's about an hour in, but I've seen it a million times, so it doesn't really matter. I love everything about this movie—the singing, the characters, and especially how slightly dorky Jesse falls for sarcastic Beca. Watching him pursue her, even when Beca shoots him down, makes me wonder what that would feel like to have someone really fight for you. And not in a scary, controlling way, but in a way that makes you believe that there is actually someone out there for everyone.

The Barden Bellas are about to perform their final number when the sound of keys jangling distracts me from the movie. I mute the TV and sit up a little, listening to the front door jerk open. There's a giggle and a deeper-sounding chuckle.

Great.

Mom's home and she's not alone. Again.

"Well, I had a really great time, Jim." Mom's voice is pitchy and lilting, like she's half-singing her words. My lip curls up in disgust. That's my cue to pull my mother back down to earth.

"Hey Mom," I call, not yet daring to move.

"Hey baby," she yells back, clearly startled. Did she really think I'd be asleep already? What does she think I am, eighty years old?

I hear a series of sharp, staccato whispers, then the sound of the front door clicking shut. Mom pokes her head into the living room. "You're still up?"

I nod, then raise my eyebrows. She yawns.

"Is Mac in bed?"

I shrug. "I think. He was playing the DS."

She shakes her head. "I'm going to have to start imposing time limits on that thing."

I don't say anything to that. Instead, I lean back against the throw pillows and watch as Jesse and Beca finally exchange a passionate kiss after the Bellas nail their performance. Mom glances at the TV for a minute, then sighs.

"Now why can't a man kiss me like that?"

I keep staring at the screen. "Because it's a movie, Mom."

"Well, I've been chasing a kiss like that my whole life." She sighs.

"That explains a lot," I can't help but mutter. I'd never

admit what I'm really thinking—that the kind of chemistry in this movie is the kind I'd love to feel in real life too. With a happy ending. Maybe even with a "happily ever after."

But I'd never, ever own up to it.

Trust me, the last thing I need is to start taking after my mom in the romance department.

FIVE

⇒ MARIJKE ⇐

Monday mornings are the worst, but since it's the first school day since we won the county track meet, I manage to drag myself out of bed with a little more enthusiasm than usual.

I yank a blue halter dress from my closet. Tommy loves it when I dress up. When we talked on the phone yesterday, I asked him about his gig at Skinners, but he seemed distracted. A few times, I was sure I could hear him typing in the background, which totally pissed me off. He knows there is nothing I hate more than being digitally two-timed.

Tommy and I met halfway through our junior year when he transferred from a private school in the city. I remember seeing him for the first time and feeling a strange queasiness in my stomach. For a second, I thought I was sick. Then I realized I was just smitten. Tommy had no shortage of girls falling at his feet and, being sort of a jock, I never thought I'd have a chance over the eternally tanned, coiffed, and lip-glossed. But Tommy said he liked my devotion to my sport and my competitive edge. He came to watch me run at every meet that spring. By the time we lost the county championship that year, Tommy and I were inseparable. We spent that whole summer in complete bliss.

Well, *almost* complete bliss.

The first time Tommy and I argued was a month after we'd started dating and I saw him flirting with Kari Caprice at a pool party. Of course he said he was just chatting with her, but everyone knows Kari's been crushing on Tommy since he moved here. Then, a few months later, I was on vacation with my family when photos popped up on Facebook of Tommy with his arm around Miranda Hoffman. Once again, he denied that it was anything romantic.

"Baby, it was a picture—don't you ever put your arm around someone in a picture?"

Which I guess sort of made sense. Not that it made me feel any better. It seems like I'm always chasing after Tommy, demanding an explanation of why he was hanging all over someone who wasn't me.

So it's sort of become, like, a *challenge* to keep Tommy. As a serious competitor, I'm hoping this dress will be another win for me. I mean, he always says I have nothing to worry about, that I'm the only one for him. But still—showing a little skin shouldn't hurt my cause.

When I come downstairs for breakfast, my parents are standing at the island talking quietly over coffee.

"Honey, you look so nice!" Mom says. I attempt an awkward curtsy.

"I figured that I should greet my fans in my formal wear."

Dad nods. "Absolutely. You must always dress the part so as not to disappoint your adoring public."

"I know, right?"

I grab a banana from the fruit bowl and a yogurt from the fridge before pulling my backpack off the hook by the door.

"I'll see you guys after school."

"No practice today?"

"Nope. We actually get a break this week."

"Okay, sweetie. Have a good day," they say in unison. I shake my head. My parents truly are *too* cute, like they've been carved out of something fluffy and pastel colored. Sometimes they are a little obnoxious in their high-school-sweetheart love. Being the by-product of my parents' relationship can be a burden too. It's a lot to live up to when you're the end result of the world's most adorable love story.

Tommy's late picking me up, which isn't a huge surprise. Since he started driving me to school, I think he's been on time a total of once—and that was the day I'd asked him to be early. We always make it to school, but my mornings usually include a mad dash to first period and, often, an apologetic smile to Mr. Pearson when I duck in a few seconds late.

In the old days, I probably would've texted one of my girlfriends while I was waiting. I used to be the student government secretary, up until last spring, and my old best friend, Courtney, is still the president. But when I had to make a choice of what to commit to as a senior, time with track and Tommy outweighed school fund-raisers and committees. Since then, I just haven't felt close to Courtney, or any of my old friends, really. Track and Tommy suck up all of my time and energy now. Not to mention school. And my far-too-perfect parents.

I pull up Facebook on my phone and start scrolling through the status updates below my profile. There's a reminder to the track team about this morning's plan—we're all meeting in front of the school so we can walk in together. I glance down the street again, then at my watch. If Tommy is too much later, I'll miss our grand entrance completely.

I continue scrolling until I see Laura Browning's tiny profile picture, with comments underneath her status post. I can see her response to a question Tommy must have asked her and his reaction.

Laura Browning: Sure. Anything 4 u, sexy.
Tommy Lawson: ;)

Narrowing my eyes, I press on her status and now I can see the entire conversation.

Tommy Lawson: Hey Laura, could u do me a favor?
Laura Browning: Sure. Whattup?
Tommy Lawson: Could u possibly bring me the calc HW today @ lunch? I'll be forever in ur debt.
Laura Browning: Sure. Anything 4 u, sexy.
Tommy Lawson: ;)

I can feel the bile rising in my throat. There's a voice in the back of my head that says, *He sent her a wink—not a smile. A* wink. *What's up with that?*

He's just showing his appreciation, I think.

But my inner voice sneers in disbelief. Appreciation is saying "thank you." A wink is full-blown flirting.

Of course, Tommy chooses this moment to peel onto my street and speed up to my driveway. I just stand there, staring at him, as he pulls in behind my dad's Subaru and hangs his head out of the window.

"Hey champ! C'mon, we're gonna miss your big entrance!"

Champ. Like what you'd call a little brother or something.

I think "champ" is the exact opposite of a wink.

Numbly, I start walking toward the passenger side of the car. Tommy reaches over and pops the door open. I pull my backpack off my shoulder and grab for the door handle, trying to figure out what I'm going to say to him.

Then I see the dozen long-stemmed red roses in the passenger seat.

"A dozen roses for my track star," Tommy says softly. He has an earnest smile on his face. I blink several times, looking back and forth between him and the flowers.

"When you walk into school, it'll be like you're at the Olympics or something," he says. "Like you've won a gold medal."

I sigh, trying unsuccessfully to tamp down the smile curling the corners of my mouth.

This is so typical of Tommy. He'll do something to upset me, to make me question everything about our relationship, and then he'll find a way to make me see how much he really cares.

Besides, everyone knows what red roses symbolize. And they mean a lot more than a wink does.

SIX

God, I'm *such* a sucker. And this unbearable kink in my neck is doing *nothing* to improve my outlook.

I try to rub it with one hand while I toss books into the boxes around me. The last two bookmobile pickups are in the next twenty minutes. I've been sitting on the floor of the Student Activities office (again) for about an hour (again) by myself (a-freakin'-gain!).

The only time I've left this room was to watch the girls' track team make their grand entrance this morning. They marched in with an entourage of cheerleaders and waved to the crowd like pageant contestants. Beth Stuart blew kisses and Katie Miller did a cartwheel and a back handspring through the front lobby. I suppose going to states *is* a big deal. Since I'm the furthest thing from an athlete, I wouldn't really know.

Last to enter the school was Marijke Monti and her

boyfriend, Tommy Lawson. I don't really know Marijke, although I've had classes with Tommy before. He's definitely one of the best-looking senior guys—and every girl knows it. I watched him bend to say something to Marijke, and she beamed up at him. In the crook of her arm, she was carrying a dozen red roses. I didn't know if I should puke or clap along with everyone else.

Now, shaking my head, I pile the boxes in two separate stacks by the door, leave a note for the bus drivers, then head for the third floor. If I'm late to first period again, I'm not sure Ms. Dotson will be as gracious as she was last week. *Twice* last week, to be precise. The elevators are on the other side of the building, so I take the stairs. Other than the slap of my flip-flops on every step, the stairwell is silent. Which is why I'm completely unprepared for the body that barrels into me a few seconds later.

"Oof!"

I'm airborne for a second, then my body slams down against the linoleum tile. There's a scuffling sound next to me and a male voice cursing under his breath.

"Wow, are you okay?"

Eyes closed, I wince and put a hand to my head, which is throbbing from the impact. Nothing seems to be broken or bleeding. I move my arms and legs to be sure.

"I think so," I say slowly, wiggling my fingers. Then I open my eyes and look up.

At Joe Lombardi.

Of course.

Of course I ran into Joe Lombardi.

Of course I'm now lying on this dirty floor, staring up at his piercing green eyes, and feeling like a total idiot.

This is the stuff that happens to me. This is the stuff I'm going to be remembered for— being a total spaz in front of the guy I've been crushing on for two years.

"I, uh, I'm sorry. I didn't mean to—" I stutter then go silent as Joe gently reaches down to help me up. His grip is firm but careful. His hands feel warm against my skin, and I want to close my eyes again.

"You don't need to apologize," he's saying, leaning over to pick up my books. "I'm the one who wasn't watching where I was going. Probably should stop texting and walking altogether, huh?"

"Maybe." I give him a weak smile and dust off my legs. "Thanks for the help."

I take my books from his hands, and he gives me a grin.

"Sure thing . . ." He pauses, cocks his head at me. "What's your name again?"

My heart falters a bit. *Figures.*

"Lily. Lily Spencer."

"Right. Lily." Joe's looking at me as if he knows me from somewhere but can't place me. I could remind him—home ec, human geography, and the half dozen other classes we've been in together. But I don't. Instead, I look down and tuck a stray curl behind my ear.

"Thanks again," I say as I start back up the stairs.

"Joe."

I blink and look back at him. He's got his hands shoved in his pockets now and he's still smiling.

"My name's Joe," he says, as though *I'm* the one who doesn't remember *him*.

"I—right," I shake my head, unable to stop the smile creeping over my lips. If I ever have to give an example of irony to someone, this will be it.

"Thanks, Joe," I say, my cheeks hot. He shrugs and starts heading down the last flight of stairs.

"Anytime, Lily," he calls over his shoulder.

Joe disappears through the first-floor entrance, and I stand there, grinning stupidly, before turning and practically floating to calculus.

He said my name.

Joe Lombardi said my name.

Now let's hope he actually remembers it.

SEVEN

⇒ MARIJKE ⇐

I really couldn't have asked for a warmer welcome. When the girls' track team marched in through the glass doors of the school entrance, at least half the senior class was crowded throughout the entrance and connecting hallways. People were clapping and whistling. Teachers were cheering from their classroom doors. I beamed up at Tommy, who was holding my hand.

"It's all for you, baby," he said over the commotion. And then he winked at me.

Which is when I remembered Laura Browning and her Facebook flirtation with my boyfriend. I looked up at Tommy uncertainly, but he didn't notice my expression. Now that we're out of the crowd and into more typical hallway traffic, I consider my words carefully.

I end up settling on, "So, since when are you friends with Laura Browning?"

"Huh?"

"Laura Browning," I repeat. We've reached Tommy's locker and now he's busy looking for his history book under a pile of papers.

"Oh, her. She's in my calculus class. Why?"

I bite my lip, trying to figure out a way to say this that doesn't make me look like a jealous mess.

"No reason. I just noticed you two were talking."

Tommy gives me a blank look. "I don't remember that."

"On Facebook."

"Oh, yeah—about homework." Tommy gives me a funny look. "Seems like you know more about it than I do, though."

I shrug. "Your convo popped up on my newsfeed this morning."

"Uh-huh."

He's smirking at me, and I feel my cheeks coloring. "Anyway," I say, trying to sound breezy, "I've got to run by the Student Activities office before class. Since I resigned my post as secretary, they talked me into running the graduation committee. I'll see you at lunch?"

"Of course."

I lean in to give him a kiss, and he pulls me in close.

"You know you're the only girl for me, Marijke," Tommy whispers in my ear. I smile against his neck. Those are the only words I ever want to hear.

Well, those words, plus three more little ones . . .

"All right, folks, move along please." Ms. Jensen, my

science teacher, is standing next to us with her arms crossed. Tommy shoots her a winning smile.

"Sorry, Ms. J. We were just saying good morning. I hope yours is lovely as well."

In spite of herself, Ms. Jensen chuckles and shakes her head.

"Let's just move along to class, Mr. Lawson. Okay?"

Tommy tips an imaginary hat to her and I just smile, looking down. Tommy's a natural-born charmer—it's in his genes or something. As my grandfather would say, "He could sell a bottle of ketchup to a lady in white gloves."

"Have a good day, baby."

Tommy grabs my hand and raises it to his mouth. He brushes a light kiss over my fingers.

"I'll see you in a few hours." Then he swings into his history class.

I walk down the hall, grinning with the knowledge that half a dozen girls are watching me with undisguised jealousy. Days like this make me think that my life is just about perfect—I'm going to states, I've got a hot boyfriend, and there's still prom, graduation, and senior week to look forward to. Everything is coming up Marijke.

EIGHT

> LILY <

I can say with utter confidence that I learned absolutely nothing in math class today. Every time I started to write an equation, I'd remember Joe's bright-green eyes or his warm, strong hands and by the time I'd broken out of my reverie, Ms. Dotson had already moved on to a new problem. Fortunately, I sit next to Bill Danner, who is a math genius—I manage to copy most of his notes, despite his nearly illegible handwriting.

By the time the bell rings for second period, I've started considering other possible ways to run into Joe Lombardi again. It's not like I could just randomly just show up at the motocross course—how totally awkward would that be?

Hey Joe . . . those are some really round tires you got there.

So, you ride here often?

What's your sign, baby? Besides, you know, street signs . . .

I. Am. So. LAME.

Groaning aloud, I turn the corner toward my journalism class. Immediately, I'm assaulted by dozens of balloons.

"What in the world?" I say, batting the ribbon tails away from my face.

A glance around shows me a handful of other bewildered students are doing the same thing. Then I see Sam Peterson standing at one end of the hall and his new girlfriend, Layla, at the other. Layla's mouth has dropped open and I can't really blame her; her boyfriend is standing fifty feet away from her wearing a full suit of armor. I don't know where someone even *gets* one of those.

I watch along with everyone else as Sam clomps toward Layla, clumsily maneuvering around the balloons. Some of their tails catch on his chain mail. As he gets closer, I see a red rose in one of his metal-clad hands. In the other, he's holding a shield with the words, I'LL BE YOUR KNIGHT IN SHINING ARMOR IF YOU GO TO PROM WITH ME.

Ugh. I should have known. Prom proposals are easily the best *and* worst part of a girl's senior year.

I don't know when the prom proposals started. What happened to guys and girls just *asking each other* to dances? In the past few years, though, no one is satisfied with a simple phone call. Now, all the guys are expected to make a grand gesture. Hence the suit of armor and balloons.

Although, as I watch Layla nod at her boyfriend before throwing her arms awkwardly around him, I feel an unwelcome twinge of envy. When I think about that kind of chutzpah, the guts it takes for a guy to announce his intentions in the middle of the school day . . . well, it's pretty admirable. Even a cynic like me can admit that.

Sam struggles to remove his helmet, and I turn away when Layla launches herself at his face. I don't know what it is about kissing—whether it's my mom and one of her many dud-dudes or two classmates or even strangers, there is little that makes me feel more wistful than a true, honest, no-holds-barred kiss. I can't think of anything I'd rather have or anything that feels more impossible to get.

All right, Lily. Buck up. Get past the balloons and the bluster and you've got an idiot wearing the contents of a recycling bin.

As I walk into journalism, I see Tricia Michaels, the editor in chief, leaning over a mock-up of next week's paper. She glances up at me, then rolls her eyes.

"You see that out there?" she sort of sneers, jerking her head at the doorway. I nod.

"Yeah."

"Whatever. I mean, I had Donavan take pictures of it and stuff. But I mean, talk about lame prom proposals. My boyfriend better think of something *way* more creative."

I don't say anything as I walk to my desk. Tricia is not exactly my favorite person—she's super-judgmental and says nasty things about the rest of the newspaper staff when they aren't around—but she's on SGA with me and heads up the National Honors Society. So she's not someone I want to piss off before graduation—not if I want to graduate with one of those NHS cords draped over my gown. And let's face it, of course I want that.

I start rummaging through the stacks of paper on my desk. This spring, I'm in charge of the Senior Sections—it's a tradition that the seniors get a special feature in each edition until graduation. We've done Superlatives and Sports Spotlights already. Now I'm working on the Senior Wills, and that means I've got about three hundred submissions to sort through. Not every senior participates in every section—but Senior Wills? No one misses out on that one. We do a double issue just to fit everyone in, and each application has a word limit.

"I bequeath my soccer ball to the girls on JV, my jersey to Coach Bruin, and my cleats to my girl, Josie. You girls are gonna rock next season," says Missy Gunner, the girls' soccer captain and all-around jock.

"To my boyfriend, Hanson, I leave all our letters, the rose petals I've saved, the pictures from the photo booth, and a thousand kisses. I will always love you, boo-bear!" says Heidi Ponce, who's been dating her boyfriend,

Hanson, for, oh, maybe a month. I have a feeling Senior Wills are kind of like tattoos—easy ways to doom relationships. But who am I to judge? I haven't even written one yet. Not that I even know what I'd say . . .

I bequeath my undying love and affection to Joe Lombardi, who knocks me off my feet in the stairwell and in life. Let's "motor" our way to the future. Vroom-vroom, baby.

Ugh. Yeah, I might skip out on this altogether.

"Hey Lily?" Gina Holt walks toward me holding a folder and wearing a determined expression. "I need you to take over this story for me."

I want to sigh in relief. *Anything* to take me away from the Senior Will purgatory I'm in.

"Sure," I say, reaching for the folder. "What's it about?"

"Prom proposals," she says before turning around. "You have to summarize the ones that have happened so far and rate them on a romance meter."

"Rate them on a *what*?"

"A romance meter," she says over her shoulder. "One kiss for 'just friends,' two for 'fun and flirty,' etc. It goes up to five—'hot 'n' heavy' or something like that."

This is what I get for complaining about Senior Wills— a prom proposal exposé complete with a rating system?

I force myself not to gag. Here it is—hard-hitting journalism at its best, folks. I'm sure my Pulitzer is already on its way.

NINE

⇒ MARIJKE ⇐

All week long, the big story at school is Sam's prom proposal. It's probably the most dramatic one that's happened so far this year. By Friday, though, I'm kind of sick of hearing about it. Sick . . . and jealous, I guess. Still no prom proposal in my world—at least not yet.

At lunch, the saga of Sam and Layla is replaced with my friend Jocelyn's story about how her boyfriend, Owen, asked her to the prom last night too. Owen's a pretty private guy, so I think we're all surprised by his renting advertising space on a movie theater screen. When Jocelyn sits down to see the most recent *Paranormal* movie, up pops a picture of Owen holding a set of cue cards and a shy smile. She shows us a picture on her iPhone where he's holding one that says, WILL YOU GO TO PROM WITH ME?

"It was so incredibly romantic," she says breathlessly.

"And the best part is that it's over now. I mean, I was dying to find out the way Owen would ask me. But now that it's done, I can focus on my dress and my hair and all the fun parts of prom. Not the stressful parts."

A couple of the other girls are nodding—most of my teammates have already been asked. Beth glances over at me and raises an eyebrow.

"Nothing from Tommy yet, I gather?"

I shrug and try to look unfazed.

"Not yet. But Tommy's a planner—I'm sure he's got something killer up his sleeve and he is waiting for the perfect moment."

The movie theater idea is pretty genius—and since Tommy's taking me to the old revival theater this afternoon, I wonder if a prom proposal is what he has planned. The fact that we're even going there is a romantic gesture—there's a showing of one of my favorite movies, *Titanic*, playing for one night only.

So that's what I'm thinking about when I meet him at the General Qi after school. He's already waiting, leaning up against the passenger-side door with his muscular arms crossed over the chest of his black T-shirt. God, he looks scrumptious. Once again, I feel that flit of hesitation, of self-consciousness—like, *Why is he with me?* I may be confident on the track, but I'm anything but when it comes to Tommy. I'm not a cheerleader or model thin or movie-star gorgeous. I'm just a girl who runs fast and loves him. But maybe, just maybe, that's enough.

"Hey baby."

He wraps his arms around me and smooths a hand down my back, then kisses my cheek.

"Ready to go?"

"Sure." I smile up at him as he opens my door and I slide inside. The smell of leather seats and vanilla air freshener hits me immediately, and I settle into my seat.

"So, did you hear about how Owen asked Jocelyn to the prom?"

Tommy frowns a little, then shakes his head.

"No, I don't think so. Definitely heard about Peterson's proposal on Monday, though. Man, he's got it bad for Layla—what self-respecting guy would rent a suit of armor and fill a hallway with helium balloons?"

"I think it's sweet," I say, pouting a little. Tommy grins at me.

"That's because you're a born romantic."

"Well," I say, giving him a pointed look, "at least Layla *has* a date for the prom . . ."

He sighs. "You know, I don't know who came up with this whole prom proposal thing anyway. What ever happened to simply asking, 'Hey, wanna go to prom? Sure, sounds good.' Seriously, why is it necessary to roll out the red carpet for a sure thing?"

I stare at him. "So that's what I am to you? A sure thing?"

Tommy glances over at me. "That's not what I meant."

"That's what you *said*."

"Come on, Mare, you know what I mean. We've been together long enough that prom should be a given, right?"

"Well, that doesn't mean a girl doesn't want a romantic proposal to get her there. Prom's less than a month away."

"Whatever. Let's just drop this. I don't want to fight with you."

We run by my house so I can feed the dog and write my parents a note. No one's home when Tommy pulls into the driveway. He pauses, shifting the car into park.

"Want me to come in with you?" he asks, looking over at me.

I swallow. There are dueling Marijkes again, just like when I start a race. One Marijke says, "Absolutely I want you to come in—I want you to do a lot more than that!" The other Marijke says, "No 'I love you' means no hanky-panky. Period."

"Do you want to come in?" I ask, meeting his gaze. His lips spread into a sexy smile.

"Well, I figured I could come inside for a little while and remind you just how romantic I can be . . ."

He cocks an eyebrow, and I feel my resolve starting to thaw around me.

"Okay," I say slowly. "But we're only staying for a minute."

We're hardly in the door before Tommy has his hands on me. I drop my bag on the living room couch just as he pulls me against him.

"Tommy," I protest as he begins to nibble at my neck.

"I thought you wanted me to be romantic?" His voice is a little gruff in my ear and a shiver passes over me.

"I just don't think we should start something we can't finish. And the movie starts in less than an hour. This is important to me."

"Okay, okay." He brushes a barely there kiss over my lips. "Then let's get out of here so I won't be tempted."

I scribble a note and leave it on the counter. When I glance over at the kitchen table, I can't help but notice the stack of papers at my place that seems to be growing every day. I've been accepted to three different universities, but I haven't officially made a decision yet. North Carolina State is my top choice and I should have mailed in my acceptance last week, but I'd been so caught up with practicing that I couldn't even stop to breathe. Now is the perfect time to catch up, but let's face it: I'm so caught up with Tommy that I haven't had the time or desire to start filling out boring paperwork.

So I leave it for another day. Again.

Instead, I focus on *right now*—on making Tommy understand how I feel about him and putting him in the position to ask me to prom. Like Jack and Rose in *Titanic,* we're meant to be together. I just know it.

TEN

> LILY <

As I leave school, I pull out my phone and hit the voice mail icon. I don't know if Mom felt bad about going out almost every night this week or if she just wants to try and reconnect, but when she woke up this morning she was determined that we have a Girls' Night In. Mac has soccer practice for most of the evening, so she promised to hit Redbox on the way home from work.

"A good romantic comedy?" she'd suggested while packing Mac's lunch. "Maybe something with Gerard Butler?"

My mom has a thing for Gerard Butler—it's actually more of an obsession than a thing. She talks to him when he's on-screen. Like, literally. Things like, "Oh Gerard, why can't you live on the East Coast?" As though that's what is keeping a famous movie star and my mother apart—geography.

There's a beep in my ear, then my mom's breathy voice.

"Hey Lil, it's Mom. Listen, I'm really sorry for the short notice . . ."

I already know what's coming, even before she says it.

". . . but Jim called and he got some last-minute tickets to see a Journey cover band that's supposed to be really good. I didn't get a chance to get movies or cook, but I've left some money on the counter. Mac is still going to Nathan's after soccer, so you can take advantage of an empty house—order pizza, hang out, whatever. Love you, call me if you need anything."

When I press end, I realize I've balled my free hand into a tight fist and my face feels hot and sort of prickly.

I'm pissed. *Really* pissed. My body just realized it before my brain did.

It's been forever since Mom and I really spent time together. I love Mac, but he's always around and he's younger, which ensures the majority of Mom's attention is directed at him. Having a night alone with her, where I could talk about things—school, grades, my insurmountable crush on a motocross racer—was more valuable than I'd realized.

That is, until I lost it.

Tears prick the corners of my eyes, and I furiously blink them back. No, I will *not* let myself get worked up about this.

No longer motivated to rush home, I decide to drive through downtown. It's one of my favorite places to be—the windows of the old row houses glow with a warmth you can practically feel. People saunter without rushing toward a particular destination. Restaurants throw open their doors and create dining rooms on the sidewalk. I love seeing the life and the vibrancy.

I'm sitting at a stoplight when I glance over to the left and do a double take. Through the window of a popular pizza joint, I see Joe Lombardi. I'm starting to wonder if seeing him is kismet or something—like the universe is trying to tell me something. Then I notice who is sitting next to him:

Mindy Kellogg. Blond and tan. Thin and perfect. And, frankly, dumb as a box of rocks.

He is laughing at something she's saying, and she reaches over to touch his arm. I feel a shudder of jealousy bolt through my body.

The truth? I can't compete with that. I'll *never* be able to compete with that.

Still, I can't get myself to look away until, moments later, the driver of the SUV behind me lays on his horn. Everyone in the restaurant turns to look, and I slam on the accelerator, speeding through the intersection like I'm being chased.

Despite my desire to run home and drown myself in Ben & Jerry's, I stop to throw some pennies in the fountain at the center of town. We've always called it the Square, even though it's actually a circular area of brick walkways and perfectly manicured grass surrounding a large stone fountain. I think of some potential wishes. Should I go for something outlandish? Realistic?

I decide on happiness as a vague but somewhat lofty goal and, with gusto, launch the handful of coins at the surface of the water. They all plop in, save one that skitters along the stone edge before falling into the abyss of a crack in the brickwork.

With my luck, that will be the one that was lucky.

The scrolling lights of the revival movie theater catch my eye. I've always loved the old-school charm of the building, which was a bank or something before they converted it. The guy who owned it was a big-time movie-industry person who grew up here. The revival theater was his contribution to the town—his legacy. He left enough money to keep it going and promptly died of some kind of overdose. That's Hollywood for you.

I'LL NEVER LET YOU GO, JACK! is scrolling across the ticker-style sign. ONE NIGHT ONLY, it says, THE MOVIE THAT MADE ALL OUR HEARTS GO ON—*TITANIC*! STARRING LEONARDO DICAPRIO, KATE WINSLET . . .

I'm a sucker for *Titanic*, and it would definitely be a distraction. It takes me about two seconds to decide that a movie is the perfect place to lose myself for a while. Taking a deep breath, I head straight for the theater doors.

ELEVEN

⇒ MARIJKE ⇐

When we get to the theater, I notice the afternoon has gotten a little chilly—colder than I expected. Tommy sees me shiver and he wraps an arm around me, squeezing my shoulders as we move toward the front of the building. I look up into his eyes, and he smiles down at me.

God, I love this guy.

"Hold up." Tommy pats his jeans' pockets. "I left my wallet in the car."

There is a line forming at the ticket booth. I don't want to miss out on getting tickets.

"I can go get it," I offer. "I'll stay warmer if I move around."

"I can think of half a dozen ways to keep you warm," Tommy says, his voice low. I grin but playfully swat at him.

"Only a half dozen? Maybe you're losing your touch."

He winks, then tosses me the keys and moves toward the back of the line.

When I get to General Qi, I grope around the space between the front seats until I feel the smooth leather of his wallet. I start to close the door when I notice Tommy's phone in one of the cup holders. Guess he will probably want that too. I lock the car and go to pocket the phone, but something stops me. I stare at the black screen and a voice in my head says, *You can just look at a text or two. It's no big deal.*

Something inside tells me not to do it, says it's a bad idea. But whatever that something is, it's easy for me to ignore.

I slide my finger across the screen and it brightens. I shake my head; I need to remind Tommy *again* to put a password on his phone. Still, I smile stupidly at the picture that's flashed up on the screen. It's one he snapped a few months ago. It was still cold enough for my winter coat, and my face is half-buried in the fur-lined hood. I'm smiling widely—a lot like I am right now. I guess Tommy just brings that out of me: complete and total joy.

Which makes me feel even worse about snooping . . .

But it definitely doesn't stop me.

I let my finger move down to his e-mail icon and then over to the picture of a speech bubble—his text messages. I look up and around as if I'm afraid he's watching. Then I tap the bubble.

There are names I recognize—me, of course; his mom; his sister; the guys in the band. I start to scroll. There's one from Lindsey Marks—they were working on a project for civics. I keep running my finger down the list, an immense sense of relief flooding my chest.

And then that relief evaporates.

There's a text from Jess Myers. Before Tommy and I got together, he and Jess had a thing. It was short, but I know she never got over him.

I take a deep breath and look back down at Jess's name.

Don't freak out, Marijke.

Don't assume the worst.

Right now, I can only see her last text to him.

Jess Myers: I guess I just miss u.

I swallow hard. If I read the whole chain of texts, will I lose it in the parking lot and go all crazy-Marijke on him?

Yes. I know that is exactly what's going to happen. And I click on the text anyway.

The screen scrolls through an endless chain of messages. From what I can see, they've been going on for months. The list stops rolling at the last few texts, and I peer down at the words.

Jess Myers: Well, Marijke just snapped u up. We nvr really got our chance.

Tommy Lawson: IDK what 2 say . . . I didn't know u felt like that.

Jess Myers: I guess I just miss u.

I suck in a breath. The two Marijkes are back—the reasonable one who's telling me to take a deep breath and calm down. And the other Marijke, the out-of-control version of me who's demanding I confront Tommy.

Why wouldn't he tell me that his ex has been texting him about getting back together? Why in the *world* would he be texting her back?

Screw this.

I clench my hand around the phone, then shove it into my pocket before stomping toward the front of the theater.

I guess you don't have to guess which Marijke I'm listening to.

TWELVE

→ LILY ←

I buy popcorn, a soda, and Sour Patch Kids. I know, I know—
dinner of champions. Between all the pasta, pizza, and junk
I've been eating lately, I'm lucky I haven't turned into a
carbohydrate.

When I enter the theater, the lights are already dimmed;
still, it's easy to navigate to my favorite seat—third row
from the back, all the way on the left. A few minutes later,
just as Bill Paxton begins speaking, the theater door flies
open, flooding the entrance with a splash of light from the
lobby. Most of the theatergoers glance up at the woman
who has sort of stumbled in. As she mounts the stairs and
gets closer to where I'm sitting, I can hear her sniffling
loudly.

When she plops down in the chair directly in front of
me, the dam bursts. Out come squeaky sobs that I think

she's trying to hold back but can't. I want to be annoyed. Somehow, though, I feel sorry for her.

"Excuse me," I whisper, tapping her shoulder. "Do you need a tissue?"

She turns to face me. Lip trembling, she nods her head. "Thank you."

And then our eyes meet, and I jerk back in my seat.

I can't believe it—the person sobbing in the chair in front of me, the person seemingly desperate and alone, is none other than Marijke Monti.

"Thanks," she mumbles, taking the tissues.

I try to focus on the screen, not on Marijke's constant sniffling. Old, wooly-haired Rose is beginning to tell the story of her teenage romance, but it's impossible to concentrate when there's an emotional breakdown occurring just two feet in front of me. At one point, Marijke blows her nose so loudly that a woman turns around and glares at her.

"How are you crying already?" she hisses. "Nothing's even *happened* yet."

Marijke manages to pull herself together, but it's only temporary. She makes it just long enough to see Jack's first glimpse of young Rose on the balcony before the dam breaks again; she pops up out of her seat with a strangled yelp, then frantically feels around for her purse. Seconds later, she half-runs, half-stumbles down the stairs and out the double doors.

Well, good. Maybe now I can actually *enjoy* the most tragic love story ever.

But for some irritating reason, I can't stop glancing over at the door and thinking about Marijke. Her devastation was just so—so *obvious*. The way her shoulders were hunched over—it was as if something had deflated inside her body. Something important. Like her heart.

I exhale a little too loudly, then get up and head down the stairs. Marijke Monti may be Molesworth High School elite, but she's still human. The least I can do is make sure she's not going to go drown herself in the coin-filled fountain.

When I make it outside the theater, it's starting to rain, but not much. It's the kind of weather a depressed person would sit in, letting the wetness permeate her clothes and mingle with her tears. Which is probably why Marijke is sitting out there right now, on a bench in front of the fountain. I can tell by the way her body is sort of shuddering that she's still crying.

I approach slowly, as if she were an animal I could spook if I made any sudden moves.

"Marijke?"

She looks up, her eyes confused. When she recognizes me—at least, I *think* she recognizes me—she sort of shatters, breaking into a new round of tears and letting her head drop into her hands.

"I'm sorry. I'm having a t-terrible night," she chokes out. When she looks up at me again, she peers at me for a second before asking the inevitable.

"I'm sorry, what's your name again?"

I sigh. "Lily. Lily Spencer."

"Right," she sniffs. "Lily."

"So, um, anyway, are you going to be okay, or . . . ?"

I trail off as Marijke stands up and runs a hand through her damp hair.

"I just . . . I don't know what to do. He just left me here. I yelled at him about the text messages, and he said I was overreacting. And then he just—he said—"

Whatever "he said" is lost in the wake of Marijke's sobbing. Sighing, I glance around the courtyard where we're sitting.

"I'm going to go grab a coffee," I say, nodding toward The Coffee Grind, a little café next to the theater. "Do you want something? We could go sit down for a minute and . . . talk. I mean, if you want to."

Marijke glances uncertainly at the coffee shop. "I guess a slice of lemon cake would make me feel a *little* better."

The Coffee Grind is warm inside and the scent of freshly roasted beans floats through the air. Once we've gotten our drinks—my large Americano drip and Marijke's froufrou frozen whipped-cream-topped monstrosity—along with a huge wedge of cake, I sit in a leather armchair. Her tears seem to have subsided as she plops down in the chair across from me and digs into the fluffy white icing on her lemon cake with a spoon. One bite later, she groans.

"This is amazing. You want a bite?"

I shake my head and she shrugs.

"Yeah, I shouldn't eat it either. Gotta stay in shape for states."

She takes another bite, then she looks up at me.

"Listen, if I tell you something—I mean, if I talk to you about some stuff, can you keep it between the two of us?"

I blink, then nod. "I, uh, sure. I mean, you don't have to say anything you don't want to."

Marijke closes her eyes for a second and exhales. Her expression is pained.

"I love the track girls. I mean, they're like my sisters," she says. "But I can't really talk to them about my boyfriend troubles. They'd just tell me to break up with him."

"Do you want to break up with him?"

"No," she says, "but I'm afraid he's gonna break up with me."

She sucks in a shaky breath before continuing.

"I found these texts on his phone that were from his ex-girlfriend, and they were all about how she wants him back. But when I asked him about it, he said that it was nothing and that I'm being ridiculous and jealous. He said that he couldn't keep having the same fight with me over and over."

She trails off as the tears begin to fall again in earnest.

"The thing is," she whimpers, "I really do trust him. I don't think he's cheating—I mean, every social networking site would explode with the confirmation of *that* rumor. I just . . . I just hate how every other girl in the school wants him. I feel like I'm always on high alert, waiting for some girl to try to snatch him away from me."

Outside, the rain has started to pick up and the drops splatter against the window, blurring the movie theater's sign into a fuzzy, fluorescent mass. Marijke reaches out and traces a heart through the fog that's beginning to form on the glass.

"What about you?" she asks, looking over at me.

"What do you mean?"

"Do you have a boyfriend?"

"Er, no. Not really. I mean, no, not at all."

She cocks her head. "But there's someone you want to be with, right?"

My brow furrows. "Why do you say that?"

Marijke shrugs.

"You've got that look."

"What look?"

"The swooning look. The love-struck look. The look that says you've been crushing hard for a while."

I blink, then look down at my hands. *She could see all that in a look?*

"Well . . ." I twirl a dark curl around one finger, "there's someone that I sort of like, and I—I've never really had the chance to talk to him much . . ."

"Who is it?"

I feel uncomfortable. "I don't know. I've never told anyone—"

"Seriously? I've been spilling my guts to you. I promise I won't tell a soul. If I do, you've already got a boatload of intel on me."

I sigh. "Sworn to secrecy?"

She nods, and I look down at my hands.

"Joe Lombardi," I whisper.

"Who?"

"Joe Lombardi," I say again, a little louder this time. I glance around the almost-empty café as if someone might have heard.

"Wow," she says, leaning back in her chair. "I'm . . . surprised. Joe is definitely hot, and he's got that sort of dark-and-dangerous thing going on. You just seem so . . ."

"Studious?" I arch an eyebrow.

"Straight-edge," she says, crossing her arms.

"Yeah, well, it doesn't really matter anyway. He doesn't know I exist."

We both look out the window then, watching the theater sign scroll through its message.

"You know what would be great? If life could be like the

movies," Marijke says with a sigh, scraping up the last bit of icing onto her fork.

"What do you mean?"

"I mean, why *can't* relationships center around big romantic gestures and sweep-you-off-your-feet moments?"

"Such as?"

"Such as you meet the love of your life and he asks you to prom in a hot air balloon or on top of a mountain or something," she suggests.

"Or the guy you've had a thing for finally learns your name and falls for you too?" I suggest.

Marijke nods. "Exactly. Is that really the kind of stuff that only happens in movies? I mean, the movies must have been inspired by real-life events, right? Think about it—*Titanic* was a horrible disaster in history, but Hollywood turns it into one of the greatest love stories of all time. That can't be a one-shot deal."

And that's when I get the idea.

If my life were a movie, you'd see a lightbulb appear over my head or a lightning bolt strike my body. Regardless of the source, inspiration hits me with a force that's practically electric—an idea that's impossible to ignore and might be just crazy enough to work.

THIRTEEN

⇒ MARIJKE ⇐

If you'd asked me a few hours ago what I'd be doing right now, I would have guaranteed it wouldn't be this: baring my soul to a girl whose name I didn't even really know until tonight.

Lily is sort of staring off into space, and I take another bite of my cake. She's the last person I would ever have expected to confide in, but it *is* actually kind of comforting to talk to her.

"What if I told you there was a way to get your wish?" Lily asks me.

I raise my eyebrows, confused. "What do you mean?"

"What if you could pick some of the strategies they use in the movies," she says. "Some of those big, mind-blowing, attention-seeking strategies—and put them into play?"

"Huh?"

Her eyes are bright. "I'm serious. If you want Tommy to

see that you're the only girl for him, you need to show him. And what's the best way to do that? Through grand gestures! I mean, if guys can make dramatic stuff like prom proposals work, why can't we pull some ideas from our favorite movies?"

I just stare at her for a minute.

"You're serious?" I finally ask.

"Yeah. What do you think?"

"I love Tommy," I say slowly, "but I'm not sure upping the drama is the best way to make our relationship work."

"But it could be," Lily argued, leaning forward. "I mean, what could it hurt? You just said that movies have to have a basis in reality. Why would it be in the movie if it was totally unrealistic?"

"I don't know . . ."

"I just think it's worth a shot."

I frown, trying to weigh my options. "Let me think for a minute."

I consider the facts. First, I hate that so many girls flirt with Tommy, and he really doesn't shoot them down as much as I'd like. I need to get him to focus on me and only me. Not to mention that I want him to love me. And I want him to say it out loud. Preferably with an audience of many so they'll know he's off-limits for sure.

But to make that happen, I know I need to try something different (especially considering that what I'm doing now isn't getting me anywhere but alone and crying in the rain).

I look at Lily as she sips her coffee. It's true that I barely know this girl, but maybe it's better that way. It's like in the movies, where two people are supposed to be somewhere else but end up in the same place at the same time and the whole plot changes because of one chance encounter.

"So we'd be in this together, right?"

Lily frowns. "Well, of course—I can help you if you want."

I shake my head. "Uh-uh. No way. If I'm going to attempt this craziness with Tommy, you've gotta do the same thing with Joe."

Her eyes grow round. "Wait a second! I didn't mean—I wasn't going to be a part of this whole thing—"

"That's the only way I'm doing it," I say, interrupting her. "If I know you've got as much to lose as I do, then we can help each other—no one would even suspect it. It's not like we're friends or whatever."

Lily cocks an eyebrow.

"Okay. So say I agreed and I said I'd do it. Does that mean you're in?"

I look at her face and I recognize that hopeful expression. It's almost like looking in a mirror. Slowly, a smile begins to spread across my face, until it's transformed into a full-fledged grin.

"Oh yeah," I say, nodding. "I am *so* in."

FOURTEEN

⟶ LILY ⟵

We stay in the coffee shop until a very irritated barista tells us they're closing. At that point, we've brainstormed maybe fifty different movies—sappy dramas, quirky comedies, indie films, eighties classics: almost nothing was off-limits. Some of the movies were mutual choices, like how we both loved *Never Been Kissed*. Other ones we had argued over— I'm dead set against Disney movies, considering most of them need magic carpets, mermaids, or singing, dancing household appliances. Marijke begrudgingly admitted that I was probably right, although I know she's still holding out for a glass slipper or magical rose or something.

In the end, we come up with a basic goal. We have three weeks before prom, which isn't much time. By then, if we do this right, Joe and Tommy will have fallen head-over-heels in love with us and we'll have Hollywood to thank for it.

"Okay, so . . ." I look down at the notebook I've been using, then back up at Marijke. "What do we start with?"

"Well, I don't know about me, but *you* need a meet-cute," she says.

"A what?"

"It's from *The Holiday*—you know, that movie where Cameron Diaz and Kate Winslet switch places? There's this old producer guy who talks about meet-cutes in the movies he used to make. It's when two people meet for the first time in a unique way, a way that makes them remember each other."

"Well, yeah," I say doubtfully, "but Joe and I have already met. We've had classes together. I've run into him in the stairwell and managed to make a fool of myself . . ."

"Yeah, but does he *remember* you? Could he pick you out of a lineup of girls with dark curly hair?" Marijke presses.

I grimace.

"Okay, I see your point."

"So there needs to be a meet-cute. A way to put the two of you together so that he'll never forget your name or your face. So that he'll be *intrigued* by you."

"And how do we make that happen? Aside from using hypnosis."

She shoots me a dirty look, then grins. "Don't worry

about that. Meet-cutes need to be spontaneous. You just leave all the details to me."

"Oh, God help me. I don't know about that . . ."

"Listen," she says, "if we're going to make this work, we're going to have to trust each other."

"Yeah, I know," I sigh. "Okay, a meet-cute it is. What's next?"

"A pinkie swear."

I frown. "What movie is that from?"

"No." She shakes her head. "A pinkie swear between me and you."

I roll my eyes. "We *really* don't need to do that."

"Um, pinkie swears are promises. And breaking them equals perjury. Gimme your hand."

Reluctantly, I reach across the table and latch my left pinkie with her right one.

"I swear," Marijke says solemnly, "that I will uphold my agreement to make our lives just like the movies. I promise to do whatever it takes, even if it's totally embarrassing, to get Joe Lombardi to notice you."

I shake my head, but I can't help the smile spreading over my face.

"Now you," she prompts.

"I swear," I say slowly, "that I will uphold my agreement . . . what was the rest?"

"To make our lives just like the movies."

"To make our lives just like the movies," I repeat. "And I'll do whatever it takes to get Tommy Lawson to fall madly, passionately in love with you and only you."

"And ask me to prom."

"Fine, and ask you to prom. But only if Joe asks me too."

"Perfect." She pulls her pinkie away, grinning. "Now all we have to do is make a foolproof plan, and there's only one way to do that."

"Oh, and what's that?"

She raises her eyebrows and gestures to our list of movies.

"A movie binge, of course—a marathon of flicks all night until we can't see straight. Until we're quoting them in our sleep. We can crash at my house; I've got Blu-ray. Whaddya say?"

Well, it's not like I've got anything to rush home for.

"Only if I can pick the first movie," I say. Marijke grins.

"Deal."

PART TWO

AND NOW, OUR FEATURE PRESENTATION

FIFTEEN

⇒ MARIJKE ⇐

I'm sort of surprised when Tommy pulls up to my house Monday morning. We didn't talk all weekend, so I'd asked my dad to drive me to school. But as Tommy rolls up, windows down and music blasting, I feel a thick, molasseslike dread creeping through my veins. It's slow and methodical, coating all my nerves with something like fear.

I can remember every second of Friday's disaster—the way my hand clenched around his phone, the way I shoved it at his body as if it were my worst enemy.

"I know the truth," I had hissed at him. "I know all about you and Jess Myers."

"Huh?"

"You heard me," I said, eyes narrowed. "I read the texts. I know she wants you back."

My fury began to boil over when Tommy rolled his eyes.

"Baby, she's harmless," he'd said. "I mean, yeah, she sent me a couple texts last week. I didn't think it was important. I don't want to get with her or anything."

To which I responded, "The least you could have done is shoot her down!"

Which is when Tommy threw up his hands and shook his head, looking at me with something like defeat.

"Why do you always think I'm cheating on you because I talk to other girls? *You* decided to look through my phone, and *you* got mad about something that is completely innocent. Talking to other girls does not equal cheating. Especially since *she* texted *me*."

"Whatever," I'd said, the hurt leaking into my voice. Tommy exhaled hard.

"Marijke, I don't touch other girls, I don't hang out with them alone, I don't go behind your back. I talk to them. I'm *nice* to them. That's it. And that's why this"—he gestures between the two of us—"clearly isn't working. Because you can't trust me, and I'm tired of trying to prove myself to you."

When he'd walked away, I was sure he wouldn't actually get in his car.

When he got in his car, I didn't think he'd really start it.

When he started it, I was positive he wouldn't drive away.

But the roar of General Qi's engine as Tommy drove away had made my heart sink to my knees. Now, the same roar has transformed to a purr as the car idles by my mail-box. I'm hesitant as I reach the passenger door. Tommy looks at me, and his mouth quirks into a small smile.

"Ready for school?"

I nod, still feeling unsure.

"I didn't know if you'd be here today," I say as I slide in next to him. He immediately puts his hand in mine and a sense of ease begins to fill my body.

"Baby," he says, curling a finger under my chin, "Friday was awful. I think we both said things we didn't mean."

I don't know what to say to that, so I don't say anything. He nudges my chin up and over until our eyes meet.

"Do you believe me when I say that I'm not cheating on you?"

I nod slowly, biting my lip. Tommy sighs and moves to put his sunglasses on.

"I'm tired of fighting with you. I've told you that you are the only person I want to be with. What's it going to take for you to believe me?"

I blink at him.

"You're right," I finally say. "I believe you."

"Thank you," Tommy exhales, smiling at me.

As he pulls away from the curb, I settle back into my seat and look out the window. His hand has moved to my knee, which he's stroking in little circles. Those circles feel like an entire solar system rotating around my body.

Tommy is here, in this car, next to me, and he's mine. I need to remember that.

When we get to school, I find Lily at her locker, poring over a textbook thicker than a brick. We stayed up until after midnight on Friday, watching all the best parts from a bunch of different movies—the kissing scenes, the fighting scenes, the I-can't-live-without-you scenes. When she'd left a little after midnight, yawning but smiling, we both reconfirmed our commitment to the pact.

"Hey, I've got a question for you."

Lily glances over at me and grins. When she sees Tommy standing a few feet behind me chatting with Doug Mason, she shoots me a questioning look.

"Is everything . . . copacetic?"

I frown. "Well, I have no idea what that means, but if you're asking me if we made up, the answer is yes."

She laughs. "While we're making over our love lives, can we work on making over your vocabulary?"

"Har, har," I say, rolling my eyes.

"By the way," she says, handing me a stapled packet of papers, "I typed up our plan this morning. I figured we should keep it organized, you know? Then I can revise it as we go."

I stare down at the title THE MOVIE EXPERIMENT in bold letters and shake my head.

"You did *this* this morning? You're going to make me self-conscious with your overachieverness."

"Well, *you* are going to make me late to class," she

counters, slamming her locker shut. "And overachieverness isn't a word."

"Listen," I say, ignoring her last comment, "I wanted to talk to you about doing a couples feature in the newspaper. Like, the love stories of the senior class. Don't you think that would be awesome?"

"I, uh, sure. I can talk to Tricia about it . . ." She glances at her watch, then back up at me.

"Why can't you just write it yourself?" I press.

"Seriously?" she asks, lowering her voice. "You want me to add a pukeworthy page of high school romances to the next edition of the paper?"

"What, you don't think the readers would eat it up?"

"Baby, we're gonna be late," Tommy says behind me.

"No, it's fine. Our classes are right here," I look back at Lily. "Well, what do you think?"

"I'm not sure," she says uncertainly, "but he's right—the bell is going to ring any second."

"Nah, we've got plenty of time!" I argue.

"Marijke—" Tommy begins.

And then it happens—he's drowned out by the screeching, alarmlike bell that marks the beginning of the school day. I can't help my grin as Tommy jumps through the doorway of Mr. Miller's history class. I can hear him call out, "I'm here—totally on time! Nobody panic!" I manage to dodge into the doorway of my first period too.

Lily, on the other hand, is at the opposite end of the hall

from her first class. I watch as she slams her locker shut and starts half-running, half-skidding when Mr. McCarthy, one of our assistant principals, rounds the corner.

"You're late, young lady," he says sternly, pointing at her.

"I—yes, I know. I'm sorry, I got . . . caught up," I hear her pant.

"You know the rules—zero tolerance for tardiness," he scolds, pulling a detention slip from his pocket and uncapping a pen. I hold back a squeal of glee.

One down, one to go.

Now I just need to figure out how to get Joe Lombardi in detention today.

SIXTEEN

⇒ LILY ⇐

I really might kill Marijke. Worst. New-friend-slash-partner-in-deception. *Ever.*

I've never had detention before. I don't even know where to *go* for detention. At the end of the day, I have to stop in the front office and ask one of the secretaries. *So* embarrassing.

When I slip into the third-floor classroom, it's empty except for two people. Mr. Marsden, the computer science teacher, is hunched over his desk, flipping through a stack of papers. There's one guy in detention with me—he's sitting at a student desk with his head buried in his arms.

"Name?" Mr. Marsden asks, looking at a clipboard.

"Lily," I say softly, so as not to wake the sleeper. "Lily Spencer."

"Right." He checks something off on the clipboard and

motions toward the empty desks. "Pick one and settle in. You'll be here a while."

I turn back around and heave my bag up onto my shoulder. When I glance around at the desks, trying to decide where to sit, my eyes lock with the now-awake student. Slowly, his green eyes crinkle and his lips spread into a smile.

My fellow detentiongoer is Joe Lombardi.

I suck in a breath but try not to make it obvious that I'm flustered. I can't believe this is happening. I don't know whether I'm mortified or thrilled.

"I know you," Joe says as I get closer. "How's the head?"

"Shh!" Mr. Marsden hushes him, scowling. "No talking!"

Joe throws him an apologetic smile. "Sorry, Mr. M—just being friendly."

"That's not necessary, Joseph. How about you focus on ways you can avoid being late to class? Then you might not land yourself in here again."

Slowly, I slide into the desk next to him. Joe smiles at me again and I smile back, willing my face to stop going all tomato on me.

"Hey," I whisper.

"Hey yourself. Fancy meeting you here."

I nod and start pulling books from my bag. Joe puts his head back down, but this time he's propped it on one arm. It takes me a second to realize that he's watching me. I glance back at Mr. Marsden, who's just put in a pair of earbuds and is rocking out to his easy-listening jams. Way to supervise, dude. I could be plotting a bank heist and you'd have no clue.

"Is that all homework?" Joe asks, incredulous. I glance at the stack of books and papers I've piled on my desk and shrug.

"Some of it. Some of it's just extra stuff for the newspaper."

He shakes his head. "I can barely keep up with my classes and here you are taking on *extra* work. If you need some more, you can always have mine."

"Thanks, but no thanks," I say, shaking my head. "I'm already almost drowning in loose-leaf paper and textbooks."

We lapse into silence and I start working on my trig homework. Or pretending to work on my trig homework, that is. I can't think when my heart is beating this hard—it's like attempting to do math during an earthquake. When the whole world is shifting around you, you're lucky if you remember your own name, let alone how to work out complex equations.

"Are you taking trig too?" I finally ask Joe. He makes a face.

"Precalc. For the second time. I suck at math."

"Math isn't so bad," I counter. "I mean, it's exact—not like English or music or something artistic. I hate when there aren't right answers."

"Well, I'm terrible at it, exact answers or not."

I cock my head and look at him. His mouth lifts up into a half smile.

"What?" he asks. "You're looking at me like you want something."

God, how am I supposed to respond to *that*?

Instead, I scoot my chair out and walk toward Mr. Marsden. He yanks out an earbud and glares at me.

"Miss Spencer?"

"I was hoping you'd let me help Joe out with his math homework. I'm really good at precalculus."

Mr. Marsden leans back in his chair and narrows his eyes. Then he shrugs.

"As long as you are working, I suppose it's okay."

I beam at him. "Thanks."

I start back toward my desk and look at Joe, who's gaping at me.

"How did you know I have precalc homework?" he asks, sounding amazed. "Are you psychic or something?"

I laugh. "No, but I've taken the class. Ms. Owens is brutal, and she gave us homework every day of the week—even over weekends."

"Sounds about right." Joe nods. He reaches behind his chair and unzips his backpack, then pulls out his math book and a spiral.

It occurs to me that I didn't even ask him if he *wanted* help—maybe I'd offended him or something.

"Sorry, I probably should have asked you if you even wanted help."

"Are you kidding? Of course you can help me out—I've got to keep my GPA up for motocross. Otherwise I can't compete."

"Well, okay then," I say, pulling my graphing calculator out of my bag. Then Joe scoots his desk closer to mine, effectively blocking me in with his body.

"Thanks for this," he says quietly. I meet his gaze and it's as soft as his voice. "It's kind of embarrassing to be this bad at something. Especially when you're repeating the class."

I swallow hard and force myself to shake my head.

"It's no big deal."

Before I realize what's happening, Joe reaches out and tweaks one of the curls close to my face. When I look at him again, he grins.

"It's a big deal to me."

SEVENTEEN

⇒ MARIJKE ⇐

Just call me Matchmaker Marijke.

Okay, don't call me that.

But still—I am *so* good at this already. Getting Lily stuck in detention was easy. The assistant principals are always prowling the halls after the bell. Getting Joe there, though, was harder. I pulled a *Steel Magnolias* and pretended I'd lost a contact on the floor and, chivalrous guy that he is, he'd done his best to help me find it. Of course, that meant he was late to third period and got a one-way ticket to Marsden's Detention Den this afternoon.

I decide to swing by the third floor and see if my grand plan is working before I head down to the track. Even though we don't have official practice again until next week, my muscles are pretty unforgiving when it comes to impromptu vacations. I have to keep them stretched and ready to

support my leaps and bounds, whether I'm technically supposed to or not.

But I let myself stop on the way outside and watch
through the little glass window in Mr. Marsden's classroom
door. I can barely see Lily, hunched over a desk, with a math
textbook next to her. Joe is poring over a book of his own,
then looks at her and says something. She reaches over and
points at something in his book, then points at his paper. He
nods and starts writing.

Seriously?

This is how she flirts—by *tutoring*? I get them stuck in
a room together and the only thing she can think of doing is
homework?

I groan aloud, then shake my head. Clearly I'm going to
need to spend more time explaining to Lily that math is the
furthest thing from sexy and no one ever caught her dream
guy by working through equations.

Minutes later, I'm tightening my shoelaces and then
peering out at the hurdles, trying to erase the distractions
from my brain. All day long, I've been thinking about what
movies to use, what scenes would work best, and how I can
get Tommy to say that he loves me.

Now I shake my head. If I'm going to run my event with
any kind of confidence, I've got to find a way to compart-
mentalize. I need to separate my running from my relationship. Closing my eyes, I imagine the shotgun start and I

bolt forward. I attempt to pull the magic act that always works best for me—dividing myself into two people. One Marijke who runs with the wind at her back and one Marijke who pauses to consider her options.

Today, it's just not working. I leap over my hurdles with a sort of resignation.

For the first time in—well, ever—running feels less like freedom and more like a job. Every hurdle is like an item on a checklist and not a single one feels like a priority. I've got to get things moving with Tommy so I can go back to being the kind of girl who moves forward, not backward. And Lily is the key, with her organized ideas to get the movie plan rolling full force. She's like some kind of smart, curly-haired secret weapon.

But I don't see Lily again until lunch on Tuesday. When she comes up to me, though, her eyes are bright and full of something like ideas.

"Say anything," she says.

I squint up at her, now leaning over me with both hands on her hips.

"Huh?"

"Say anything," she repeats.

"Um . . . anything?" I try, attempting to follow her clearly insane logic.

She rolls her eyes and plops down on the ground next to me. I decided to bypass my usual lunch table today in favor of the spring air. That, and I know that Posey's boyfriend, Jeremy, asked her to prom at last night's tennis match—I heard something about him spelling out "PROM?" in plastic cups pushed through the chain-link fencing around the courts. It's a cute idea, really—I just can't really handle hearing someone else's adorable prom proposal story today.

Lily drops a DVD in my lap.

"*Say Anything*," she repeats. "The movie. That's how you're going to get Tommy's attention."

I look down at the case. A young John Cusack stares up at me.

"Of all the movies on the list, you had to choose the only one I haven't seen yet?"

"Trust me," she says, tapping the plastic box, "this movie is a classic. And it's got the most iconic display of true love that's ever been in a movie."

"Iconic?"

"Yeah, iconic—well-known, major, important . . ."

I snort. "Overdramatic much?"

But Lily's shaking her head. "No, seriously—you've probably seen it before. John Cusack standing outside a car, holding a boom box over his head. The song 'In Your Eyes' blasting from the speakers. Ringing any bells?"

I shrug. "Maybe. I'm not sure."

"Well, if nothing else, just check out the boom-box scene on YouTube. It's epic."

"Okay, okay." I tuck the movie into my bag. "Speaking of epic, how was detention with Joe Lombardi yesterday?"

Lily's normally pink complexion deepens into a blush. "How did you know about that?"

I grin. "Let's just say I had my reasons for making you late to class yesterday."

Lily blinks at me, her gaze blank. Then her eyes widen. "You did that on purpose?"

"Maybe . . . ," I say coyly.

Her face morphs from shocked to sort of impressed.

"Wow. I might actually hate you a little less now. How did you get him there too?"

"Same way, really. Made him late because he was helping me find my contact lens."

Lily peers at me. "I didn't know you wear contacts."

I shrug. "I don't."

"Right. Of course you don't." She shakes her head, then she sighs.

"Detention was . . . nice, weird as that sounds. Talking to him was nice and sitting with him was nice and everything was really . . ."

"Nice?" I offer. She leans back on her elbows and looks up at the cloudless sky.

"I just don't know how to be anything else but a tutor or the SGA secretary or a school newspaper columnist. I don't know how to make people see me as something other than . . ."

"A nerd?" I supply. Lily gives me a dirty look.

"Stop finishing my sentences. And no, not a nerd. More like a . . . a resource. I don't want to always be *that* girl, the one who's just there to help."

"So then, what did you guys talk about in detention?" I ask. She bites her lip.

"I, uh, helped him with his math homework."

"Exactly—and you wonder why he only sees you as a walking textbook? It's because you make yourself one. Come on! You've got to put yourself out there!"

"Marijke, it was *detention.* We weren't supposed to talk at all. The only way I could was if we were doing something academic."

I sigh, zipping my backpack and sliding it over my shoulder.

"Okay, okay—so tell me about this *Say Anything* scheme. What exactly would I have to do?"

"Is that your way of telling me you aren't going to watch the movie?"

"Maybe."

Lily groans.

"Fine—in the movie, this guy Lloyd wants to get this girl Diane back after they broke up, so he stands outside her window with a boom box and blasts a superromantic song. So I'm gonna run to the A/V office to see if I can snag one of those portable iPod docks they use in the auditorium. The ones with the Bose speakers? I think that would be perfect for this."

I blink. "Wait—you seriously want me to hold a speaker dock up in the air, outside Tommy's house, with music blasting?"

"Well, unless you have a boom box and it's really 1985, then, yeah, I think the iPod dock is probably our best bet."

"I—I guess I thought the scene wouldn't be so . . . I don't know, totally mortifying?"

Lily stares at me.

"Was that not clear about this being the most romantic scene from the most romantic movie ever? You would be a legend if you pull this off!"

"I guess so," I say, swallowing. I pause for a second. "Look, the only way I'm doing this is if you do something for me."

"Oh yeah? What is that?"

I cock an eyebrow at her and grin. "You're going to be my wingman."

EIGHTEEN

⇒ LILY ⇐

A good-size iPod speaker dock with high-quality speakers and a remote control costs hundreds of dollars.

I know this because Mr. Dylan, the teacher in charge of the audio-visual department, told me no less than four times in the ten minutes I was in his office.

"Now, if I let you borrow this," he said, "I will expect it back within twenty-four hours and in perfect condition. These things cost hundreds of dollars, you know."

"I think you mentioned that," I say dryly.

"Well, all right then." He slaps the thighs of his jeans and stands up, peering at the shelves lining the room. "You said it needs to be battery operated, right?"

"Yes, please."

He yanks a sleek black unit down off an upper shelf and sets it on the table in front of me. Quickly, he points out the basic anatomy—where the iPod goes, how to control the volume, how to switch or shuffle songs. When I finally manage to get out of there, it's with one more warning about being careful and I'm already ten minutes late to fifth period. Fortunately I weaseled a late pass out of Mr. Dylan—no more detention for me, thank you very much.

After school, I make it home in record time. I want to race and get on the computer before Mac gets home from school and demands to use it, allegedly for homework but actually for gaming. Mom isn't supposed to get home until six, so I'm a little surprised to pull up at three thirty and see her car in the driveway. Cautiously, I let myself into the house.

"Mom?" I call out uncertainly.

"Up here," is her muffled reply.

I follow the sound of her voice, scaling the stairs to her bedroom and pausing in the doorway. She's in bed. I can see she's got on her fuzzy pink bathrobe and her hair is a strange combination of frizzy and flat.

"Are you okay?" I ask, alarmed. "Are you sick? You look awful."

"Way to kick a girl when she's down," Mom sniffs, grabbing another tissue. That's when I notice the red eyes and forlorn expression. I'm pretty sure I can guess the cause, but I go ahead and ask anyway.

"What happened?"

She chokes a little on another bout of tears, then manages to say, "Jim dumped me."

Sighing, I sit on the edge of the bed, fingering the lacy edge of her comforter. I say what I know she wants to hear.

"I'm sorry."

"Yeah." She sniffles again. "I really thought he might be *The One*, you know? A nice guy, good with kids, the whole package. But of course, once again I'm reminded of why the male species sucks."

I laugh at that and she manages a smile.

"What did he say?" I ask.

She deepens her voice into an impression of Contractor Jim.

"I just see myself starting a life and a family with someone younger," she drawls. "And baby, you already got a few too many miles on them tires."

I gasp. "Tell me he didn't actually say that!"

She nods miserably.

"Well, then he's a loser, Mom. And it's better that you find it out now before things could have gotten more serious. God, who says stuff like that anyway? How old is *he*?"

"Thirty-eight."

"Right. Like he has any room to talk—he's three years older than you!"

"Yeah, a little less, I think. He's a Gemini. I should have

seen it coming—those Geminis always have dual person-
alities. It's impossible to tell what they're thinking."

At one point, my mom thought it would be a great idea
to start learning about astrology. She probably hasn't studied it in, oh, about eight years, but she'll still talk about it as
if she's been giving readings in a tent with her crystal ball
nearby.

"I'm sorry, Mom," I say again, trying to sound genuine and patting her hand. I move to stand. "Do you need
anything?"

She shakes her head. "No, nothing for me. If you can
keep an eye out for Mac, though, that'd be great. I just want
to make sure he gets in and does his homework before getting on that godforsaken DS."

"Sure."

I'd expect nothing less. Mom needed time to mope alone
with her broken heart. Still, the slow burn of bitterness
crawls up my chest and into my throat like vomit. I hurry
out of the room before I say something I'll regret. Something like, "How about you get over yourself and act like a
mom?" or "Maybe it's a good thing Jim dumped you—now
you can stay home and parent for once."

When I make it back downstairs, I slide into the computer chair and wiggle the mouse to wake up the monitor.
Above me, I can hear Mom moving around. The creak of
her mattress. Footsteps padding across the floor toward the

bathroom. I sigh and pull up Google Chrome. I need to focus on *Say Anything* and Marijke's scene tonight.

I'd be lying if I said it hadn't occurred to me that, by helping Marijke, I might really be trying to help my mom. I mean, not that what I'm *doing* will help her, but Marijke's about as pressed on Tommy as my mom gets on her Man of the Week.

I shake my head. Doing this—the movie thing—was my idea and I'm going to see it through. And after seeing Mom, broken and bed-bound by her heartache, I know I don't want that for Marijke. I actually do want her to be happy.

I guess she's kind of becoming my friend. Which is totally weird.

And, of course, there's the Joe factor. Marijke's detention tactic was pretty slick. Especially since I didn't know about it—it made it all the more real, the more special, when he and I talked and studied and smiled. I will never, ever forget the way he reached out and touched my hair. I think it took me another minute or two to start breathing again.

So I pull up iTunes and download "In Your Eyes," then I transfer it over to my iPod. I fiddle with the speaker dock, plugging the cords into the iPod, then playing with the volume.

Now it's time for the most important test.

I take the dock outside to the picnic table and turn the volume all the way up, wincing at the almost painful sound.

Man, I really hope the neighbors aren't home. I hurry back into the house and listen closely. From the living room, I can hear the lyrics loud and clear. As Peter Gabriel sings about wanting to run away and driving off in his car, I can decipher every word.

Perfect. That means that this strategy is as foolproof as possible. As long as Tommy's home, he'll hear the music. Assuming, of course, that Marijke can manage to have the courage to pull this off. I'll be the first one to admit it—doing something like this will take an awful lot of nerve.

"Lily!"

Whoops. I forgot about Mom.

I move to the bottom of the stairs to see her standing at the top with one hand on her hip.

"Lily, what in the world are you doing? Why are you blasting music outside?"

"Uh . . . school project," I call up to her before heading toward the back door. The last thing I'm going to do is tell my mom about our movie master plan. Next thing I know, she'd be showing up at Jim's house with a boom box.

NINETEEN

⇒ MARIJKE ⇐

Before I go down to the track to practice, I swing into the band room. It only takes a few seconds to find Tommy— he's in one of the soundproof booths, singing into a microphone and strumming on his acoustic guitar. He doesn't see me, so I stand there for a minute, just watching him.

God, he is just so beautiful. His skin is tan and yummy like some kind of caramel dessert. His eyes are icy blue, and yet they completely scorch me when I look at him.

Speaking of those eyes, he glances up midcroon and sees me, then grins. I move to open the door as he pulls off the large headphones he's wearing.

"Hey sexy," he says, pulling my hand until my body is pressed up against him.

"How was the chemistry test?" I ask, kissing his cheek. He smiles at me.

"I think I did really well. I mean, of course, this is my second time taking it after completely bombing the first one, but I'm feeling pretty good about it."

"That's great." I reach over and let my fingers strum lightly along the strings on the neck of his guitar. "So, listen, do you have plans tonight?"

He shrugs. "I have to go by Jimmy's to pick up an amp. Other than that, I should be home. Why?"

"I—uh—I'm just curious," I shake my head, trying my best to look casual.

Tommy slides his hand up down my back and lets it rest on my hip. "Why? You thinking about coming over to visit? Sneaking into my bedroom and surprising me in the middle of the night? I won't say no, I promise."

I can feel my cheeks coloring. "I'm sure you wouldn't."

"Hey, we could get started right now, if you want. That's the beauty of a soundproof room, babe. You can't hear out and they can't hear in." Now he smooths his other hand over the thigh of my jeans. "It's the perfect place if you wanna get rowdy."

He winks and I squirm away from him.

"Right—um, have you forgotten the huge glass window in front of us?"

He grins again and pulls me into his lap, nuzzling my neck. I let myself relax into him a bit, feeling the warmth of his body against mine. Then I sigh.

"I've got to go stretch," I say, disentangling myself from his arms. "I'm gonna get a ride home with Beth, okay?"

"Sure, baby. I'll text you later," he says, sliding the headphones back on.

As I walk out the door, I glance back and see him singing and playing again. This time his eyes are closed and my heart turns into something overflowing. It squeezes around itself. Watching him do something he loves so much reminds me of why I love him. His commitment to his music is something I can't deny or ignore. And maybe he'll see *my* commitment to *him* through music too.

Only mine is a means to an end—and that end is going to happen tonight.

In his backyard.

With an iPod dock over my head.

And my heart on full display.

I'm halfway across the student parking lot when I see Courtney Mills walking toward me. I can feel a lump in my throat, but I force myself to swallow hard.

Courtney and I used to be friends—*best* friends. All through middle and high school, we did everything together. Student government, honors society, all of that stuff. She never ran track with me, but we still spent a ton of time together—at least until Tommy entered the picture.

Once Tommy and I were a couple, Courtney and I just didn't see each other as much. Then the texts stopped. After a while, I dug myself out of my new relationship long enough to notice that I'd been replaced by Meagan, the new SGA vice president. She and Courtney were always attached at the hip. When I tried to talk to either of them, they seemed like a package deal.

"Hey Marijke," Courtney is saying, smiling at me. I glance past her, but there's no Meagan tailing her. I smile back.

"Hey Court. How's it going?"

"Oh, you know," she waves a hand. "Always busy—prom and graduation to plan for. All that stuff. Congrats, by the way. About heading to states."

I just nod, watching her face. I remember when we went ice skating for the first time and she fell against the rink wall. You can still make out the tiniest scar underneath her nose.

"How's Tommy?" she asks, eyebrows raised. I blink a few times.

"I, uh, oh, he's great. Thanks."

"Well good."

The silence is awkward between us—especially because back when we were little you couldn't get the two of us to shut up when we were together. I miss that, I realize all of a sudden.

"Listen, Court, I was wondering—"

"Hey Courtney, let's go. Nadia is waiting for us to start the meeting."

Meagan comes up behind Courtney and I feel my heart sort of sink. In another life—my old life—I'd be the one going to the meeting with Courtney and she would have been the one scheming with me about all these movies. Not with Lily, a girl I've basically just met. A girl I barely know at all.

"Later, Marijke," Courtney says, giving me a little smile. "Good luck with states."

"Later," I echo.

I watch them walk away, arm in arm, and I try to remember what I have to be grateful for. My friendship with Courtney is my past. I need to focus on my future—my track friends, my running, and my boyfriend.

Most of all, my hopefully foolproof plan to capture his heart tonight for good.

TWENTY

> LILY <

"So, let me get this straight . . ."

We're standing in the foyer of Marijke's house and she's staring at the speaker dock looking doubtful.

"I drive to Tommy's," she's saying, "park down the street, sneak into his backyard, turn this thing on, and—what? Just stand with it over my head, waiting for him to hear me?"

I shrug. "Yeah. That's about it. Why, were you expecting fireworks?"

"No, not necessarily. I just think that when guys put themselves out there like that, it's totally romantic. When a girl does it, she just looks like a stalker."

I frown. "Who cares what it looks like? Who is going to see you besides Tommy?"

"Well, you are, for starters. I already told you, I'm not doing this without you as my wingman."

I arch an eyebrow. "So, what, am I going to be holding your hand or something?"

"Nope, I've already figured it all out. It's gonna be dark out and Tommy's backyard is practically a jungle. I got my dad to bring home one of the portable spotlights they use for presentations at the dealership. I figure you could put the spot on me so Tommy could see me—so he'd know it was me and not some crazy person."

Huh. Guess she's really thought this through.

"I suppose I can do that," I say slowly. "And now that I think about it, I should probably drive too—Tommy won't know my car if he sees it accidentally."

"Good idea. Come on, let's go upstairs. I need outfit advice."

"Seriously?"

"Yes, *seriously*—come on."

When we get to her bedroom, I glance at the outfit choice that's spread out on her bed: a tight black mini and a pair of sky-high silver stilettos.

"Um, well, I would imagine Tommy's backyard is made of, you know, *grass*. If that's the case, you aren't walking any-where in those spikes—they'll sink right in and stay there."

"Good point, good point." She dives back into her closet and brings out a pair of glittery flats and a jean skirt.

"You are wearing a shirt too, right?"

Marijke rolls her eyes.

"Obviously."

She picks up a black cami from her bed and shakes it at me.

"Okay, so, a skimpy tank top and tiny skirt . . . and what exactly are you trying to make happen? A lap dance?"

"Har, har." But Marijke now looks doubtfully at her new outfit choice, and I can't help but laugh.

"It's going to be dark. Who cares what you're wearing? Just get dressed so we can get out of here. I have to be home by eleven."

It's a quarter to nine when we finally make it back down the stairs.

"Mom? Dad?" Marijke calls. I follow her as she walks into the kitchen. We both stop short when we see her parents. They're standing very close to one another and are talking quietly, with serious looks on both of their faces.

Marijke arches an eyebrow at them. "I'm going to finish studying at Lily's house."

"Not too late, okay?" her dad says, glancing at the clock.

"Okay."

"Good night, sweetie," her mom says, her voice almost sugary and oddly fake.

As I back down the driveway, I feel obligated to say something, so I go with, "Your parents seem really nice."

Marijke snorts.

"I love them, really. But sometimes they are just . . . too much."

I'm not really sure what that means, but I don't ask questions. Who am I to judge someone's parents when my mom is probably nominating herself to be the next Bachelorette as we speak?

Instead, I let Marijke direct me toward where Tommy lives, a few miles outside of town. The farther we drive, the bigger the houses get. When we finally pull into Tommy's neighborhood, I'm gawking at the McMansions and whistling through my teeth.

"Wow. I don't think I knew there were houses like this outside of the *Real Housewives*."

Marijke laughs. "Tommy's family is loaded. His dad's a surgeon and his mom's some kind of ad executive. They make tons of money, but they're never home."

"Wow. I had no idea he was rich."

She shrugs. "He tries to hide it—vintage car, used guitars, that kind of thing. I don't think he really wants people to know the truth."

"So will Tommy be the only one there tonight?"

She shakes her head. "I think Tommy's sister is home from college for a couple weeks. And his parents *could* be home, but I'm hoping he hears this before anyone else."

I hope that too. Otherwise, this could get pretty freaking embarrassing for everyone involved.

We move farther into the neighborhood, where the houses back up to a thick line of trees.

"Okay, go ahead and park," Marijke says, directing me over the grass. "His house is down at the bottom of the cul-de-sac. We can walk from here."

I carry the spotlight, which is sort of like a glorified flashlight but bigger. Marijke grabs the speaker dock with my iPod already hooked up. Quickly, we shuffle down the road in the dark. The houses are far enough away from the street that there's little light revealing us to anyone who might be watching. It's one of those kinds of neighborhoods without street lamps or sidewalks.

I gotta admit, Tommy's house is pretty amazing. Nothing like the thirty-year-old ranchers and split-levels in my neighborhood. It's blue, I think, although it's dark so it could just be blue in the dim light. There are numerous windows and a fancy front door. Above it, a stained-glass panel catches the porch lamplight and shoots a golden-rosy glow out into the world. There are a few cars parked in the driveway. Tommy's is closest to the garage, with a little two-door BMW parked behind it.

"Good, he's here," Marijke breathes. "And that's his sister's car. So hopefully his folks are out."

I just nod as we move around the side of the house. For a split second, I consider the intelligence of this idea—these are the kind of houses with alarm systems and security cameras. I wonder if someone is catching us on tape right now and simultaneously calling 911. I try to shake the thought from my head.

We won't be here long enough to get arrested, I tell myself.

Then I force myself to believe it.

Marijke has me stand in the very back of the yard, where the trees get thick and the underbrush clings to my jeans and twists around my ankles. She stands about fifty feet in front of me, roughly in the middle of the lawn. As she reaches to push play on the iPod, I stop her.

"Wait—what am I supposed to do? I mean, if he comes out and you guys are all, like, romantic or whatever."

She shrugs. "You can stay or you can go. He can take me home if you want."

"Fine. Just don't forget I'm here when you start groping each other."

I wave a hand, signaling for her to go ahead and start the music. I fiddle with the spotlight and it flashes on just as the first loud notes of Peter Gabriel's song burst from the speakers.

I look back up at Marijke, who is standing there with total confidence—shoulders back, head held high, speaker dock far above her head. I feel an overwhelming sense of pride—she's really rocking this.

I have a little trouble getting the spotlight on her and

she glares back at me, only to have me practically blind her. But once I've got it steady, I take a deep breath and watch the upstairs windows, waiting for some sign of life. Honestly, it's kind of hard to see with the spotlight's aura glowing around me. All I can really see is Marijke, sort of swaying now, as the song moves into the iconic chorus.

I can't believe he hasn't heard the music yet. I drop my arms and try to regain some feeling in them. In the air, Peter Gabriel's voice croons about light and heat and being complete. Peering up at the house, I force myself not to give up. Instead, I shove my arms back in the air.

After another minute passes, though, I'm beginning to feel doubtful. That is, until two pale figures emerge from the darkness. I don't have any trouble seeing who they are. Or who they *aren't*, really.

They *aren't* Tommy.

I hear her talking to them, and she signals for me to come closer. I kill the lights and stumble out of the wooded area, my eyes adjusting to the darkness around me.

"This is Lily," she says as I approach. I can hear her voice quavering a bit. "She's a friend of mine from school. Lily, this is Mr. and Mrs. Lawson. Tommy's parents."

TWENTY-ONE

⇒ MARIJKE ⇐

Seriously, I have never been more horrified in my entire life.

Seeing Tommy's parents last night and then trying to explain how I was doing a project for school? For *film study*, no less—a class I don't even take? I know they must have seen right through my excuses. At least they were nice enough to let me leave without too much fuss. Because, of course, Tommy wasn't home.

Apparently, *someone* had come to pick him up.

And that *someone* had been female.

Mrs. Lawson said she was the girlfriend of one of his bandmates and that she'd been taking Tommy to Jimmy's house for practice. But now, in the light of day, all I can think about are the facts. I knew this last night, but I wasn't about to face it: none of Tommy's bandmates *have* girlfriends.

They're all completely, totally single—and apparently he's acting like he is too.

I feel like I haven't slept, which frankly I haven't, and I look terrible. I don't even bother attempting to spruce up the disaster that is my appearance. I throw on jeans and a sweatshirt and head out for school while my hair is still wet and my makeup is lying unused on the bathroom counter.

I didn't say much to Lily when she took me home last night, but I did ask her to come back this morning to pick me up. She comes about fifteen minutes earlier than Tommy usually does. I did that on purpose, obviously, so we wouldn't cross his path. She's sitting in the driveway when I come outside, and I don't look her in the eye as I slide into the passenger seat.

She doesn't say anything for the first few minutes. Finally, out of the blue, she asks me, "Why don't you drive?"

I shrug. "I could—I took driver's ed. I just never took the test."

"Why not?"

I look out the window before answering her. "Because Tommy always drove me everywhere."

"Oh."

Lily stays quiet after that. Even when we get to school she doesn't say a word, but when we get to the front door, she turns to me with a worried look.

"Are you sure you don't want to just skip it today? I can take you back home—if I've got to come late, it's not that big of a deal."

Lily strikes me as the kind of girl who isn't normally tardy. Or *ever* tardy. Except, of course, when I make her late and land her in detention. I shake my head.

"No, it's fine. I need to face him eventually. At least if it's here, I won't kill him."

I give her a rueful smile before she pulls the door open.

"Well, at least you're not a sobbing mess like at the theater," she remarks.

I glare at her and she shrugs.

"Hey, just trying to point out the positives."

I'm actually starting to feel a little better. Chatting with Lily gives me something to think about other than the elephant named Betrayal that's stomping around in my head, just to remind me it's there.

Of course, any relief or distraction I was feeling evaporates when I walk to first period and see Tommy leaning on the lockers outside my classroom door. When our eyes meet, I suck in a breath, but I refuse to look away. His blue eyes look somewhere between frustrated and annoyed.

That lights a fire right under my anger. What right does *he* have to be mad at *me*?

I jut out my chin and attempt to walk past him without a word, but he's faster than I am. Moments later, he's standing in front of me with his arms crossed, totally blocking my path before I can dodge around him.

"Marijke? What's going on?"

I glare up at him, trying to ignore how sexy he looks right now. His hair is a little rumpled, like he's been pulling a hand through it in irritation. He didn't shave this morning, and he's rocking that shadowy scruff I love. He's wearing the navy-blue button down that I bought him last Christmas. I steel myself against the onslaught of a lust/ love one-two punch.

"I have nothing to say to you," I bite out. "Just let me go to class."

"No way—not until you tell me why you stood me up this morning. I sat in your driveway for almost fifteen minutes until your dad finally came out and told me you'd already left. What's up with that?"

I stare at him. "Seriously? You're pissed because I went to school early? How about I start listing all the reasons I am absolutely, totally *furious* with you?"

"Bring it on, baby. I haven't done anything wrong."

I cross my arms now too. "So leaving your house last night with some random girl to go to Jimmy's—you think that should just be okay with me?"

His brows furrow in confusion. "Wha—?"

"Yeah," I interrupt, feeling a sick satisfaction at showing him up. "Didn't think I'd find out, did you?"

And then he does something that absolutely infuriates me—he laughs. Out loud, wide-mouthed guffawing kind of laughing. I could deck him.

"Babe," he says, shaking his head, "it wasn't a random girl. It was Shelley. Shelley Lipmann."

Now I'm the one with a furrowed brow. "Jimmy's sister?"

Tommy nods. "She and her husband are staying with Jimmy's family for a week with their kids. Jimmy had her come pick me up because I couldn't get the General to start."

"But—but your mom said . . ."

He cocks his head. "When did you talk to my mom?"

"I—I was—last night I—"

I stutter and stumble over everything I'm thinking. Tommy's mom could have easily gotten her information wrong . . .

"Marijke, look at me."

Tommy curls a finger under my chin and tilts my face up until our eyes meet. I can feel the awkward embarrassment from mine meet the concern in his.

"Babe, you've *got* to find a way to trust me. Seriously, I feel like a broken record here. I'm sorry if you got the wrong idea or whatever. I spent the night at Jimmy's because we practiced until after midnight. I lost track of time, so I crashed. But I was at your house this morning, just like I always am."

I blink a few times, then swallow hard.

"I'm sorry. Your mom—did you talk to your parents today?"

He shakes his head, but his gaze turns suspicious as I exhale hard.

"Why?" he asks, eyes narrowed.

"It's not important. Forget it."

"Okay . . ." He sounds less than pleased, but the bell rings and we've got no choice but to book it. Before we enter our classrooms, Tommy pulls me in against him and kisses me hard. He moves his hands to either side of my face and looks me in the eye.

"You are my girlfriend. You're the *only* girl for me. Stop worrying so much."

If only it were that easy.

TWENTY-TWO

 LILY

"So did you see him?" I ask Marijke as I sit down next to her at the lunch table.

"Yeah, I saw him. He said it was Jimmy's sister that picked him up. Jimmy's very married-with-two-kids sister, who is in town this week."

"Oh yeah?" My eyebrows raise. "And . . . do you believe him?"

She bites her bottom lip, looking a little sheepish. "I do . . . but only because I called Jimmy's house a couple minutes ago and his sister answered."

"Oh wow! Did you actually *talk* to her?"

"Yeah, I made up some lie about Tommy thinking he left his math book there. She couldn't find it, obviously, but said that she didn't think he brought a book with him when she picked him up last night. So that's when I knew for sure."

"Wow." I shake my head. "Well, that's great, right? I mean, we wasted an awesome movie moment, but he clearly isn't cheating on you."

She sighs. "Yeah. I'm pissed that the iPod thing didn't work out, though. I mean, all that effort . . ."

"We'll figure something else out."

"Speaking of something else," she says, "I have to tell you about my new idea for your Joe-tervention."

"Shh!" I hiss, glancing around us. She rolls her eyes.

"Come on." She stands up and tosses her apple core in the trash. "We'll talk while we walk. I want to go check out the track anyway."

"Why can't we just sit and eat lunch like normal people?" I grumble, snatching my lunch sack off the table.

She shrugs. "Getting your blood moving makes your brain work harder."

Once we're outside, Marijke digs into her bag and hands me a flyer. I squint at it.

"Bikes for Tykes?" I read. "What is this?"

"Joe and his uncle are setting up this big charity event and all the money goes to buying bikes for underprivileged kids. One of the track girls gave me this a few hours ago—Joe's looking for volunteers to help organize everything. I think they're going to try to bring in a couple professional riders too."

I blink at the flier. "I'm surprised that I didn't hear

about this already. It seems like something the SGA would have jumped on."

"Well, I think that's part of the reason he's looking for volunteers—the school wouldn't approve the event. They're holding it at the track over on Route 75."

I stare at the paper, confused. "So what does this have to do with me?"

"Remember *Footloose*?"

"Yeah."

She spreads her hands wide for emphasis. "One of the best parts about that movie, besides the dancing, is that Ariel and Ren fall in love by working together to plan a senior prom."

"Right . . . so what?"

"So you'll get to Joe by helping him do something he *believes* in. If you volunteer and put yourself out there, provide all your crazy organizational skills and put them to good use? He'll see how amazing you are, and you'll be irresistible."

I look at her doubtfully. "I don't know anything about motocross."

She groans. "I'm not asking you to ride a motorcycle. I'm asking you to do what you already do best. I mean, don't you put together half the SGA events as it is?"

"I guess."

"So then you just have to find Joe and tell him you want to volunteer. That's it."

When we finally reach the track, the gate is already unlocked for the gym classes. Marijke pulls the lever up, and I follow her through.

"What are we doing out here anyway?" I ask, glancing around. "What does 'checking out the track' entail, exactly?"

She doesn't answer as she leans down to touch the tips of her fingers to the brick-colored surface.

"Um. Are you becoming the Track Whisperer or something?"

She shakes her head. "It's hard to explain. The track—it sort of . . ." She trails off, then shakes her head. "Never mind."

But now I'm interested. I rock back on my heels and cross my arms over my chest. "No, tell me. The track sort of what?"

She sighs. "It's sort of alive. It expands and contracts. It holds water one day and gets dry and brittle the next. The air and the weather decide the best running conditions. Coach is letting me come out here and train this week, even though I'm not supposed to—I'm supposed to be resting. But I promised not to get hurt, and running on a slippery track is an easy way to break that promise."

When she looks back up at me, I grin at her.

"You really know this stuff," I say admiringly. "I mean, I get that you're a good runner and it's your sport and all—but man, you've got it down to a science. You should study it—I mean, *really* study it. In college."

"Study what? Track surfaces?"

I shake my head. "No—sports management. Or something like that. You know what makes athletes better and you know how to help them. That's a pretty awesome trait."

Her cheeks begin to color. "I guess so. I should probably decide what college I'm going to before I decide on a major."

I feel my eyes grow wide. "Marijke. Seriously? It's almost May!"

"I know, I know. I have to go back through the pros and cons before I settle on one."

"Well, what are the cons?"

She shrugs. "I like North Carolina State a lot—and they've got a great athletic training program."

"Sounds right up your alley."

"I know—it's just really far. And since Tommy's going to stick around to keep the band together, I'm thinking maybe I should just hang out. Go to community college for a few years or something."

I narrow my eyes. "NC State is a really good school. You'd give that up for a guy?"

She swallows hard. "Of course not. I mean, I just think that my relationship should play a factor in my decision . . ."

She trails off, knowing she's just proved herself wrong. I can feel my lip curl in something like disgust.

"Marijke, I mean this in the nicest possible way, but that's ridiculous. And it's totally weak."

She just blinks at me and I shake my head.

"I *hate* when women throw away opportunities for the men in their lives. Why would you do that? Why would you want to be less successful just to be with someone? Shouldn't he support you with what you want to do?"

I know my tone is sharp. Marijke wheels around and stares at me.

"What's up with you?" she asks, bewildered.

I close my eyes and exhale hard. Then I speak slowly, choosing each word carefully before I say it.

"Let's just say I have close personal experience with the end results—my mom isn't exactly selective about choosing the men in her life, and a lot of those men are losers who aren't worth her time."

She opens her mouth to defend herself, then closes it. I've never talked to her about my mom before. When she starts walking up the hill again, I follow her, unsure of what to say next.

"Look, I'll talk to Joe, okay?" she says over her shoulder.

"Huh?"

"I said, I'll talk to Joe. I'll tell him we're coming to the interest meeting tomorrow afternoon and that we want to volunteer."

I blink, then I give her a small smile.

"Thanks. Honestly, it's still kind of hard for me to just go up and talk to him."

"Yeah, I know." She elbows me. "But you'd better get used to it. And fast."

TWENTY-THREE

⇒ MARIJKE ⇐

I think I'm going to have to literally remind Lily to breathe. It's about ten minutes until Joe's motocross interest meeting; even though the school isn't involved, we're meeting in one of the computer labs at the far end of the science wing. Right now, though, Lily and I are sitting in the library as she takes deep breaths and tries to focus.

"Lily?" I can't help but cross my arms and tap one foot impatiently. "Are you chickening out?"

She shakes her head. "No, I'm fine. I'm just . . . nervous."

I grab her hand, heaving her up to standing.

"Don't be nervous. We're gonna walk in, listen to Joe, brainstorm some ideas, sign up for a committee or whatever, and leave. Easy-peasy."

I try to make it sound effortless. I know that my confidence isn't enough to pull her through, but I hope it'll boost her up a bit. We head out the library door and into the hallway. Still, she walks slowly, hesitating to turn the corner toward the computer lab.

"Think *Footloose*," I whisper in her ear. "Falling in love while fighting for a cause."

"Somehow, I don't think this is the same thing," she mutters. "It's not like we're in a town that outlaws motocross the way the town in the movie outlawed dancing."

"Um, yeah, but the school isn't a huge fan of motocross. I've even heard rumors that the administration is trying to get the whole program disbanded. Trust me, this is *totally* the same thing."

I guess she takes my word for it. At this point, we're steps away from the lab and I can hear a bunch of voices speaking at once. Before Lily can take another deep breath, I yank her into the room. She almost trips over her own feet in the process.

There are about twenty people or so sitting at the rows of computers. On the far left side, Joe is chatting with a couple of kids from Drama Club. I hear the words "performance" and "dancing," to which they all nod enthusiastically. I notice the website posted up on the whiteboard and, like everyone else, I take a seat at a computer and open the Internet browser.

Once I've typed in the website, a flashy screen pops up showing a motorcycle zooming around a track that looks like a galaxy—stars swirl up and scatter like smoke around the tires. As the bike disappears, the stars weave together to form the words "Bikes for Tykes: Give Kids a Chance to Ride" in a jagged script. Then the whole image fades into a more traditional site, an "About" page followed by details and ways to donate.

Lily's at the computer next to me, looking at the exact same screen.

"I'm really impressed by the layout," she says quietly. "If Joe is this tech-savvy already, he may not need nearly as much help as he thinks he does."

"Thanks for coming, everyone."

Joe has moved to the front of the room and I give Lily a nudge. Not that she needs a reminder to pay attention. She shoots me a dirty look, then faces forward again.

"I appreciate all of you showing up today," Joe is saying. "I've really waited until the last minute to ask for help, which is super-stupid of me, but we weren't really sure we had the Route 75 track until the end of last week. The event is two weekends from now and we've barely scratched the surface of public interest. We need to find a way to get people psyched about Bikes for Tykes."

He turns around and gestures to a screen on the wall. There's a small remote in his left hand; he presses a button and the same website I'm looking at flies up on the screen.

"This is our website: the one, good, professional thing we've got going on right now. My uncle's publicist put it together for us and it totally rocks. The problem is that my uncle can't officially attach his name to this fund-raiser. It's considered a conflict of interest with some of his sponsors, or something like that.

"Anyway, the publicity we'd get from my uncle being part of the project would be amazing, but since he can't be, there's almost no traffic to the website and even less talk about the event online. I want to find a way to get the word out and get people excited about this."

He stops talking and glances around the room. I look around too. It seems like everyone's waiting for him to continue, so he raises his eyebrows and says, "So—anyone have any good ideas?"

There's a long, awkward pause and then Lily clears her throat.

"Social media."

Everyone, including Joe, turns to look at Lily. She swallows hard, then stands up.

"I—uh, I mean, you need to use social media," she stutters, wiping her sweaty hands on her jeans.

"We have a Facebook page, if that's what you mean," Joe offers. She shakes her head.

"No. I mean, yeah, that's a great start. But what I meant is that you need a social media *buzz* going. Like, to get people talking about the fund-raiser. You should have someone posting every day, multiple times a day. It could be reminders or fun facts or whatever."

Joe is nodding, and he leans over a desk to write something down. He glances back up at Lily.

"What else?"

She cocks her head, like she's considering the options. "A Twitter handle would be good. You could have some hashtags assigned—#bikesfortykes, for example. Again, you'd need someone manning it daily."

"And you'd need to send friend requests on Facebook," I call out. "Get people to add you or like your page or whatever. That way you'll start circulating more."

Joe's eyes are bright as he continues to scribble our ideas down. "Okay—Twitter handle, friend requests . . ."

He looks back up at Lily again.

"What else, Lily?"

When Joe says her name, she gets this silly grin on her face and I watch Joe's green eyes flash with something—curiosity, maybe? Amusement?

She clears her throat again.

"Well, there's always door-to-door—going out to the people and forcing them to look you in the eye. Real live people are always harder to say no to."

"Which reminds me," Joe says, gesturing to the Drama Club members he'd been chatting up earlier, "Winnie and Rob have an awesome idea to drum up interest. And I don't think anyone will see this one coming . . ."

TWENTY-FOUR

 LILY

"A flash mob!"

Marijke's still bowled over by Joe's description of dozens of people breaking into simultaneous dancing to raise interest in Bikes for Tykes. He's scheduled a meeting for early next week so the Drama Club would have time to decide when and where and what dance they want to perform. I'm a little skeptical, honestly. We really don't have much time to orchestrate a Twitter campaign, let alone a flash mob. Still, Marijke's blown away by the whole concept.

"It is such an awesome idea," she's saying, her eyes wide.

"I think you might be overestimating our resources," I warn.

Marijke shrugs. "It never hurts to brainstorm."

"Speaking of which," I say, lowering my voice, "how do you think the meeting went?"

She brightens immediately and beams at me.

"You were totally awesome—the social media thing is so key. Now that they've got someone running the Facebook page and setting up a Twitter handle, I think we'll get people fired up in no time."

"I hope so."

"Although . . ." She trails off, and I raise my eyebrows at her.

"What?"

She shrugs. "You just aren't really your snarky self around Joe. What's up with that?"

I shrug too. "I don't know. I guess I don't want to come across as mean or something."

"Yeah, but that attitude is part of who you are. It makes you interesting. And funny."

I snort. "Yeah, I'm just a regular laugh riot."

"See," she says, pointing at me, "that's what I'm talking about. You gotta be confident enough to be the real you."

"I guess."

As we head out to the parking lot, I notice a huge truck parked on the side of the road. You can't really miss it—it's one of those 18-wheelers that heave themselves along the highway as they make their way east or west. The front cab, though, is bright pink and the body of the truck has an enormous picture of senior Philip Johnson, grinning, with a rose caught between his teeth. Next to him, in curly script, are the words, "Jalina, will you go to prom with me?"

I notice the crowd now, gathered around the truck where Philip is standing, wearing what I can only assume is supposed to be a "truck driver" uniform—some kind of coveralls with a name tag. He's grinning now like he is in the picture. I follow the direction of his gaze and see Jalina Preston bounding up the hill toward the truck and him. She dives into his arms with a muffled shriek and the entire crowd starts clapping and whistling in a approval.

I glance over at Marijke, who is staring up at the truck like she can hardly believe it's there. As though it's some kind of mirage. Then she blinks sadly and looks over at me.

"It's like every time I forget about these stupid proposals, I see one that's bigger and better than the last."

"Yeah, I know." I give her a half smile and yank on the strap of her backpack. "Let's get out of here. Wanna stop and grab some ice cream?"

She shakes her head. "Tommy's supposed to pick me up in ten minutes or so. I said I'd go to band practice with him and watch them play."

I raise my eyebrows, and she shrugs.

"I figured showing that I care about what he cares about is a good idea."

"It's not a bad one, anyway," I admit. "Is that a movie tactic or a Marijke original?"

She shrugs. "I'm sure it's in a movie somewhere. For a while I was thinking I would try some kind of 'fighting as foreplay' thing, like in *The Ugly Truth* or *The Cutting Edge*. You know, how it makes them develop insane chemistry?"

She runs a hand through her hair, then squints up at the sky as if waiting for something to fall. I wonder if it's answers or a divine intervention she's hoping for.

"Anyway," she continues, "now I think fighting is the *last* thing Tommy and I need to do any more of."

"So what's your plan then?"

She grins. "Well, a flash mob—obviously."

"Right. Okay, good luck with that."

I glance back at the truck and the crowd of people, now starting to disperse. I shake my head.

"You know, not everyone is really that creative. I mean, obviously Philip knows what a girl wants, but I bet half the guys in school are cursing him. I mean, how do you top that?"

Marijke nods. "Yeah, there should be, like, a service or something. We provide the prom proposals, and you make them happen."

I stop in my tracks and stare at her. She looks back at me, brows furrowed. "What? Was it something I said?"

"Yes, it was *totally* something you said, because you are a freaking genius."

I barely even say good-bye as I dash to my car. Marijke's given me the perfect idea to raise funds for Bikes for Tykes. I just need to figure out how to pull it off.

I wait by Joe's locker the next morning, feeling the same queasy, butterfly-like feeling that I felt yesterday before the meeting. I don't know what he's going to say about my idea. He might think it's stupid or ridiculous or impossible. But I know that we could get some serious cash by doing this. I know that it will work—and maybe it'll be memorable enough to make Joe think of me when it happens.

"Lily?"

I turn to see him behind me, both hands shoved in his pockets. His eyebrows are high on his forehead, framing his questioning gaze.

"What's up?" he asks, leaning against the bank of lockers next to him.

"I, uh, I got this idea yesterday. After the meeting. I did a little reconnaissance and I think we can pull it off. And I think, like a flash mob, it'll attract a ton of people . . ."

"Oh yeah?" Joe looks intrigued. "Lay it on me."

I clear my throat. "So, you know how the prom proposals have become a really big deal? I mean, every girl wants one, right?"

He snorts. "Yeah, and for most guys, it's the worst part of the whole prom scenario."

"Exactly. So say you could take all the drama and

planning out of it—if someone did all the work for you? Set up the scene? Bought the flowers? Wrote the script?"

Joe nods. "Yeah, I think I know some guys who'd totally be into that."

"Which is why I think we should do it—advertise the perfect Moto-Proposal."

His brow furrows. "What do you mean?"

I pull out my spiral and show him the notes I've jotted down.

"See, we could advertise a prom proposal that would take place at the Bikes for Tykes event. Guys could buy raffle tickets to try to win the proposal, then a few days before we draw the name and set it up. We will keep it a secret about who the winner is, so you can pretty much guarantee that every girl without a prom date will show up at the track that day."

Joe is grinning now as he looks down at my spiral.

"This is a great idea. Did you come up with this on your own?"

I shrug. "I just came up with the basic plan. I'll need you to figure out how to pull it off. Does the track have billboards or signage or something? Is there a way to make some kind of prom proposal spectacle in the midst of the event?"

Joe is looking up at the ceiling, a thoughtful expression on his face.

"I can come up with something. Just leave the details to me."

He looks back down at me, still smiling.

"This is genius, Lily, seriously. Will you tell the others to spread the word about the raffle? We can start selling tickets on Monday after school."

I nod, smiling back at him. Somehow over the course of this conversation, my fluttering stomach has given way to inexplicable confidence. It's a pretty amazing feeling.

Almost as amazing as when Joe's hand grabs mine and squeezes.

"You are a total lifesaver," he says. "I totally owe you one."

I consider what Marijke said about being my "snarky self."

"I'm gonna hold you to that," I quip and Joe grins before letting my hand go and leaning back to look at me.

"So what about you?"

"What *about* me?"

"Have you gotten *your* prom proposal yet?"

I laugh so quickly that I almost choke on my intake of breath. "No. No balloon-filled hallways or suits of armor have shown up in my world, unfortunately."

He smiles down at me again, but this time his lips are pressed together, covering his perfect white teeth.

"Huh." Joe cocks his head and regards me. "Well, good to know."

The silence between us is palpable, and I blink multiple times as I look up at him.

"I'll catch you later on, okay?" he finally says. "Maybe we can brainstorm some more about the raffle. Will you be around at lunch? Want to meet me in the cafeteria?"

I shift from foot to foot, cursing myself for being so fidgety. "Uh, sure. I can do that."

He beams. "Great—I'll see you then."

"Right. See you then," I echo.

When I start heading down the hall, I try *really hard* not to turn around and look at him. But in the end, I give in to what my body really wants and I glance back over my shoulder.

Our eyes meet.

He was watching me go.

Something delicious curls in my belly and I smile until it hurts. I couldn't have planned this better if I'd scripted it myself.

I grin all the way to class before the truth of what I've become sinks in. Have I really become the kind of girl that lets a guy influence her happiness? Wasn't I just talking about how I hated stuff like that? Inwardly, I can't help but groan.

Freakin' Marijke.

She must be rubbing off on me more than I thought.

TWENTY-FIVE

⇒ MARIJKE ⇐

"So, guess who I'm meeting up with?"

I turn to see Lily behind me, shooting me a sly grin. I grab my tray off the cafeteria line.

"Let me guess, could it be a certain motocross god who is super-hot and really nice?"

"Perhaps . . ."

Then her mouth spreads into a smile and I follow her gaze. I see Joe sitting at a table with a handful of other guys—the motocross team, I think. He must have seen Lily too, because he gives her a nod, then crooks his finger and motions for her to come closer.

"That's a pretty sexy move right there," I whisper to her. "I wouldn't keep him waiting if I were you."

"I think you're right," she murmurs, then grins at me and heads toward him.

I let my eyes follow Lily as she reaches Joe's table and he scoots over to let her sit down. She drops her backpack on the seat next to her and pulls out a spiral notebook.

Of course—well, I guess a type A personality doesn't change her stripes. Or something.

And speaking of stripes . . . I cock my head, still looking at Lily but paying closer attention to her outfit. I think she could really use a fashion intervention. Her pinstriped, button-down shirt is like something my dad would wear to the office. While her jean skirt isn't terrible, it's about half a foot longer than I wear my skirts. I plop down at the track table next to Beth, considering ways I could get Lily to make over her physical appearance. I have a feeling that calling in the professionals of *What Not to Wear* or *Fashion Emergency* wouldn't go over too well with her.

Suddenly, my line of vision is blocked by a herd of drama kids moving past us, singing some random song from some random musical. I watch them as they head for a table in the back of the cafeteria and I'm reminded of Joe's flash-mob marketing ploy. Flash mobs are the kind of thing that everyone notices and talks about, not to mention films on their cell phones. There was that one on *Oprah* with the Black Eyed Peas. That went viral. Even movies are getting in on the act—like *Friends With Benefits*, where Justin Timberlake's character uses it to get Mila Kunis in the end. Totally adorable.

I just need to figure out how to pull one off.

After school, I force Lily to meet me at my house with an excuse about Joe's fund-raiser. When she gets there, though, I hustle her up to the bathroom before she can make a quick getaway.

"What do you mean a makeover?" Lily asks. Her tone is an equal mix of hurt and terror. I reach out and pull on the cuff of her shirt.

"Lily, this is something you wear to the office, not to school. I'm not saying you need a complete overhaul. I'm just saying that you could use a little sprucing up."

"You make me sound like a landscaping project," she grumbles. I shrug.

"Well, I can take some clippers to your hair, if it'll make you feel better."

"Ha-ha."

Once we get up to my bedroom, though, Lily turns out to be pickier than I expected. First I thought I'd give her outfit approval and allow her some sort of vote when it came to her new look. When she reached for a pair of jeans and a T-shirt, however, I realized that I'd need to veto anything she approved of.

"Just think about *Easy A*—remember how Olive got all dolled up in lingerie to get attention? And it worked!"

"Uh, if by 'worked' you mean people thought she was a prostitute!"

"Never mind. We're doing this my way. Get in the bathroom."

"You're so bossy today," she says, flashing me an irritated look, but she moves toward the hall bathroom without any more resistance.

Once she's settled on the stool next to the sink, we both peer at her reflection. Her hair is dark—really dark—and her curls are haphazardly arranged to frame her face. Her blue eyes are bright but sort of lose their luster underneath prominent eyebrows and so much hair. She needs two things really badly—tweezers and eyeliner.

"All right, we're starting with the painful part first."

"Painful?" Her alarm is back and I pat her shoulder.

"Not really. Not terribly painful, anyway. It'll just be a little pinch."

"What are you going to do to me?" she almost whispers.

"Tweeze you. Your eyebrows are a monstrosity."

"Thanks a lot."

"Hey, just keeping it real." I lean in to get a better view while I work.

Lily actually handles it pretty well, and it isn't long before I've managed to craft a clean arch and thinner brows altogether. That alone makes all the difference, but I know that eyeliner is gonna be a game changer.

"So listen," I say, rummaging through my box of eye makeup, "I forgot to tell you the details of my flash-mob plan for Operation: Tommy's Love."

Lily's newly shaped brows fly up in surprise.

"Keep still," I scold her.

But she ignores me and shakes her head.

"You were serious about that?"

"Of course!"

"How in the world will you pull that off?" she asks. I grin.

"I talked to Chelsea Norton after lunch—she's captain of the dance team. *And* I talked to Brett Yanno—he was one of the drama kids at the meeting, remember? Anyway, the Drama Club and the dance team have been working on the choreography for the musical, so they've already got a dance down pat. I asked them if they'd be willing to do a spur-of-the-moment performance, and they were all for it."

"Did you tell them what it was for?"

I shrug. "Nah. I guess they'll figure it out when they see me and Tommy making out like crazy in the middle of all the dancers."

Lily exhales hard. "Wow. I think that might be more ballsy than the *Say Anything* plan. You going to dance with them or just observe?"

I sigh, sweeping a shimmery shadow over her brow bone.

"Well, originally I was going to dance with them. But they know the steps and I want to have them perform tomorrow, so there's no way I could learn all the moves by then."

"Tomorrow?" She sounds equally surprised and horrified. "Jeez, when you decide on something, you go all out, don't you?"

I shrug. "What's the point in waiting? Now close your eyes so I can line them."

Lily makes a show of rolling them first, but then she closes her lids and I lightly draw a line along her lashes with a dark-brown liner.

"You know I'm never going to be able to remember how to do this," she warns as I move to the other eye.

"Sure you will. It isn't complicated. Besides, you're going to like it so much that you'll want to know how to do it yourself."

"Whatever you say."

I know she's still doubting me, even after I've swept bronzer over her cheeks and a sheen of pinky-gold gloss over her lips. It isn't until she opens her eyes and looks in the mirror that she finally gets what I'm trying to do.

"Wh-what did you . . . how did you do that?" she says, stumbling over her words. I grin at her in the mirror.

She looks phenomenal. The blue in her eyes sparkles now with the delicate brown frame around her lashes. Her lashes themselves look doubly long with a bit of mascara, and her lips glisten with a "kiss me" pout.

"You're lucky you have such great skin," I tell her, running a powder brush over her nose. "I didn't have to do much at all and you look outstanding. Do you like it?"

She nods, turning her head from side to side to check out her face.

"Dude, I totally owe you an apology. You were right."

I laugh. "I wouldn't say that yet. I haven't picked your clothes out, and you might not feel the same way when you see how short my skirts are."

She grimaces, but now she's a little more amenable when we move back to my room. She even tries on a sassy, strapless pink dress that I wore last summer to a concert.

"I could never pull this off," she says, her eyes wide.

"Well, you're wrong, you look killer. But it's important for you to be comfortable."

We finally settle on a short ruffled skirt with tiny flowers, a white tank top with a healthy amount of cleavage, and a cropped white denim jacket.

"I'm showing an awful lot of the girls, don't you think?" She gestures to the deep V-neck of the shirt. I shake my head.

"Nope, I *don't* think. Here's the thing—guys want to see just enough that they know there's something there to look forward to."

"So you think there's something to look forward to here?" She gestures to herself as if she's some kind of science experiment.

I take a good look at Lily. She's pushed her hair back from her face, showing off some dangly earrings. Her makeup is still perfect and looks even better on her now that she's smiling. The jean jacket and skirt have the right amount of opposing style—the practical denim versus the frilly ruffles.

"I think Joe is going to swallow his tongue when he sees you tomorrow. And I think you're going to need to find an excuse to take that jacket off and really show him what he's missing."

Lily's cheeks redden, but she looks pleased. She turns back around to look at the mirror, and she shifts back and forth to see the skirt swirl around her legs.

"Thanks for this," she says, glancing over at me. "Seriously. I owe you."

"Oh yeah?" I say. "Wanna join a flash mob?"

She snorts a laugh.

"Not in a million years."

I shrug, then grin at her. "Eh, it was worth a shot."

TWENTY-SIX

 LILY

Ugh. I feel like an absolute idiot.

I tug at the hem of Marijke's ruffled skirt. I can't believe she convinced me to wear something this short. And this tank top? It's tighter than anything I've ever put on, including bathing suits. I've never felt more self-conscious. And yet, here I am, standing in the parking lot at school, trying to muster up the courage to walk inside for my SGA meeting.

"Lily?"

I turn to see Courtney behind me. She's positively gawking at my outfit.

"I—" She blinks at me, then shakes her head. "I didn't think it was you at first, but then I saw your car. You look . . . different."

I look down again at my skirt. "Bad different?"

Courtney laughs. "No, not at all. I've just never seen you dress like this."

I shrug. "I guess I just wanted to try something new."

But when we reach the Student Activities office, Courtney's reaction is magnified by two.

"Holy cannoli, Lily!"

Meagan's face is agog as she stares at my skirt. I feel the red flush spread over my face again.

"Jeez, it's just an outfit," I mutter.

Ms. Vincent, our advisor, is sitting at the long meeting table. She just raises an eyebrow.

"Uh, yeah. A *hot* outfit." Meagan is shaking her head. "Well, someone is clearly trying to tempt a member of the student body. Who's the guy?"

I shake my head. "No one. I just figured I'd—I don't know . . . Can we just start talking about prom planning?"

Our meeting is short, considering most of the details are fairly surface level—the junior class has volunteered to organize the refreshments and the decorations are pretty standard: streamers, strobe lights, the works. I remember the Bikes for Tykes raffle at the very end, but I wait for Ms. Vincent to head back to her office before I mention it to the other girls.

"So by the way, Joe Lombardi is having this motocross fund-raiser—have you guys heard about it?"

Courtney nods. "Yeah, someone said something about

it yesterday. Apparently they wouldn't let him hold it on school grounds."

"Right. The event's gonna be at the MotoTrak across town. Anyway, listen, there's this raffle . . ."

I explain the prom proposal plan and watch as eyes begin to light up around me. The class secretary, LeeAnn Gardin, is grinning and nodding emphatically.

"That is an AMAZING idea—and I know *so many* guys who will totally go for that. I mean, I'm waiting and waiting and waiting for Denny to ask me to prom. If someone took the work out of it, I might not be waiting anymore."

"Yeah, that's the worst thing about prom proposals," Courtney says, nodding. "So many guys wait until the last minute to pull off something totally awesome. Either that or they can't think of something cool enough to do on their own."

"Exactly," I say, shuffling my feet and moving toward the door, "so we're going to sell tickets after school on Monday in the student parking lot."

"What about at lunch?"

I shake my head. "No dice—there are too many teachers around. I don't know if they'd approve or stop us, but considering their feelings about motocross, I figure we should keep this under wraps."

"Sure." Courtney's nodding and heaves her backpack on her shoulder. "Hey, speaking of lunch, why don't you come sit with us today? We can decide whether we want to get a band or a DJ for prom?"

I blink at her.

Could this friendly attitude really be because of an outfit change? Are girls really that shallow?

"Maybe," I say, trying to sound noncommittal. "I've probably got to catch up with Marijke. We've got a . . . project we've been working on."

"You two are like peas and carrots lately," Meagan observes. I pull the door open and give her a backward glance. I can see Courtney frowning behind her.

"You know how school projects are—time-consuming. They take total commitment. And I really want to ace this one."

* * *

At the end of the day, I duck into the journalism room and hurry toward my desk. We've all promised to put in some after-school hours to try to finalize our last senior issue. I flop down in my chair and I dig into the pile of Senior Wills that are threatening to swallow my desk whole.

Well, I made it. A new look and a lot of double-takes and turned heads, but I didn't change into the jeans I'd stashed in my backpack. I would never admit it to Marijke, but I'm feeling pretty proud of myself.

The only thing is, well, I never saw Joe today. Considering

the school day is just about over, the chances are pretty slim that I will.

Not that it matters or anything . . . I guess. But I mean, if I'm gonna wear a skirt the size of a *dish towel*, I should at least get to impress the guy I'm interested in.

I shake my head. What am I becoming? When did I get to be so blatantly boy crazy?

I've almost managed to forget my Joe focus and immerse myself in my task when I hear a muffled boom coming from outside in the courtyard. Everyone around me looks up and a few people run to the window.

"No. Freaking. WAY," I hear someone say. I stand up, hastily tugging my skirt into place, and move across the room to look outside.

Marijke's grin is the first thing I see, probably because it's so wide and bright that it's impossible to miss. Then I take in the fifty or so dancers moving in perfect synchronization and the gathering crowd of people that are lining up along the fringes.

I can't believe it.

She actually pulled off a flash mob.

When I glance around, I notice that most of the room has cleared out—most likely to join the rest of the students who are spilling out into the courtyard. I move quickly, hoping to make it out there before the crowd gets too dense to push through.

Marijke's standing in the same place when I finally make it to her. She's still smiling, but I can see her eyes flicking over the crowd. I don't have to ask who she's looking for.

"Not here?" I ask her. Her smile begins to falter. Around her, the dancers spin and leap along to a bass-heavy Nicki Minaj track.

"I told him this morning to meet me here. I don't know where . . ." She trails off, reaching into her pocket for her phone. She peers at the screen, then groans.

"I can't believe this."

"What is it?"

Her face morphs into a combination of frustration and fury.

"He went freaking paintballing with his friends. Jesus, all I want is for him to show up for *one* of my plans."

Suddenly, Marijke begins to melt. Literally, it's like all the air leaves her body and the tears begin to pour down her cheeks. I haven't seen her like this since the night at the movies when we'd come up with this crazy idea in the first place. Looking at her now, I'm starting to wonder if this was all a big mistake.

"Come with me."

I grab her hand and yank her through the crowd, ignoring the stares that follow us as we push between bodies.

"I really thought most people would be gone by now," she chokes out. "I didn't think I'd cause this big of a scene."

"Don't worry about it. We can say it was a performance to drum up interest for the state meet or something." I hope that will calm her down. But she shakes her head, the tears continuing to stream over her face.

"And I did all of this—made this huge scene—for *nothing*. He's not even here."

The school hallways are completely desolate now. I lead Marijke into the journalism room and then farther back to the editor in chief's office. I close the door behind us and gesture to a chair next to the wide wooden desk. She drops into it without a word, sniffling and wiping her eyes.

"Look," I say, leaning up against the desk and facing her, "we knew this whole thing would be a risk, you know? Don't let this get you down—we'll find the right game plan. The *perfect* one."

But Marijke looks totally defeated. She raises her gaze to meet mine.

"I'm starting to think this was a huge mistake. I mean, I just keep putting myself out there. And it hasn't paid off once."

"I know," I say quietly. "So maybe you should just abandon the strategies for now and just tell him the truth. Tell him you love him. Tell him what you want from him. Maybe that's all you really need to do—be honest."

She looks at me for a long time, then surprises me by standing up.

"Can you take me to the paintball arena? It's over by the mall."

"I—uh, sure. Let me just grab my bag."

I know Tricia will be pissed, but screw it. I can deal with her wrath later. The least I can do for Marijke right now is take her to see Tommy. Especially since her movie plans have turned out to be such a complete disaster.

Mine, on the other hand?

Well . . . I think they're actually working.

TWENTY-SEVEN

≫ MARIJKE ≪

So I guess it probably isn't a surprise that I've never been paintballing before.

Honestly, I'm really not sure what I'm doing here at all. As we were driving over, I thought about that cute scene in *10 Things I Hate About You* when Kat and Patrick have that competitive and adorable game of paintball. Now, though, as I watch Lily's car disappear down the road, I'm starting to think this might be a bad idea. Tommy's asked me to go paintballing with him at least a dozen times, but I feel like I'm breaking some sort of weird guy code by busting in on his game.

I take a deep breath. I don't really have a choice now. I'm here, I'm stranded, and Tommy's inside. My tears have long since dried and only left behind hurt and anger. Right now, today, at this minute, I'm done playing games.

Except, obviously, for paintball.

I throw my shoulders back and stride into the small, shedlike office boasting a fluorescent OPEN sign.

"I want a gun," I blurt out.

The gray-haired man behind the counter gives me a once-over, then raises an eyebrow.

"You got a group you're playing with?"

I blink. "Um, yeah. They started earlier. I got here late."

I look down at the guy's name tag then back up at his face and give him a smile.

"Gene—that's your name, right?"

"Yes, ma'am."

"Well, Gene, I completely spaced out and forgot to bring a change of clothes. You wouldn't happen to have something I could wear other than this, would you?"

"Of course. This is a full-service operation." Gene grins and leads me to the back. Before long, I've suited up in a pair of mechanic-like coveralls.

"Now, you'll need one of these," he says, handing me a black-fabric-covered helmet, "and some gloves. And the gun, obviously."

He lets me choose my paintball color and I pick red—red like my heart, red like Valentine's Day, red like love. It seems appropriately symbolic.

Gene consults a computer monitor, then hands me a map. "The boys look like they've made it past the ridge and they're in the wooded lot. You got the element of surprise since you're a late addition. I bet you'll get a few of them knocked off before they even know what hit 'em."

We walk out back and he gestures to a line of ATVs. I blink at them, then at him.

"I need to drive one of those?"

"Well, yeah, unless you want to hoof it for the three miles you have to go."

I look at the ATVs again. I mean, they have four wheels, right? It shouldn't be too hard. Just like driving a car.

Of course, I don't do that either, so . . .

"Don't worry, girlie, you'll figure it out." Gene sends me a wink that makes me shudder a little, then he throws me a set of keys.

"Don't you want a copy of my license?"

"Nah, I trust you." He motions down the line of vehicles. "Last one on the left. And good luck."

I'm not great at reading maps, but it's pretty easy to figure out where the tree lot begins—since, you know, it's where the trees begin. I pull the ATV over into a shallow ditch, and I feel a swell of pride. No driver's license, no experience, and I still drove this baby like a champ. If I was feeling anything other than confident before, it's been replaced with a feeling of triumph that's coursing through me like adrenaline.

Considering I've never been to the paintball arena, I don't really know what to expect. I try to approach it the same way I've seen Tommy play the first-person-shooter video games—slowly, quietly, and with lots of attention to my peripheral vision.

Gene warned me that all of the guys would look the same—the same gray coveralls, the same helmets. The only thing that would be different is the color of the paint they're shooting. Carefully, I step through a space between two trees and creep through the thickening underbrush. When Gene said "tree lot" he meant "really dense forest with lots of vines to trip on." I stumble a bit, then curse. If I'm going to be any good at this paintball thing, I'm going to have to be quieter. And more careful.

Because, apparently, that's what I want right now—to be good at paintball. To impress Tommy. I know it isn't just about paintball—that it's about his friends and his music too. But paintball is one of Tommy's go-to activities to blow off steam or have a good time. I can't help but wonder when the last time was that *we* had fun together. When's the last time we laughed and joked and let ourselves go?

Because that's the thing I feel like we're missing. We aren't just dating. We're also friends. Or at least we used to be.

And I'm going to prove to him that we still are.

Don't get me wrong, I'm still gonna unload a gallon of paint pellets at him for missing the flash mob and standing me up. But maybe that plan had been too over the top, too in-your-face. Maybe this is the way to go to get to Tommy's heart—by being part of something he loves to do.

A rustling sound has me drop down on all fours. I don't have time to question my instincts before I see a splat of yellow paint against a tree about ten meters away. Suddenly, a shadowy figure jumps up to standing and returns fire against Mr. Yellow. His ammunition is blue and he's a really quick shot. I hear a muffled groan, then Mr. Blue bounds across the open space and disappears.

I take a deep breath. Somehow, I don't think either of those two were Tommy. Which means he's still out there in the depths of this forest and it's my task to find him and take him down. I literally can't wait. For the first time ever, I'm excited to fight with my boyfriend.

Tommy's a clever guy, but I've got something on my side—the fact that he has no idea I'm here. I see him long before he sees me, even though he's in the last place I'd expect: wedged between the thick branches of a tall tree, about fifteen feet off the ground. I don't know how he made it up there, aside from shimmying up the length of the trunk. I lie in the undergrowth and watch him watching for the other players. The sack of black ammunition swings from his belt and he holds his gun like someone who knows what he's doing. It's pretty sexy.

I watch him load his paint pellets and take aim at something—or someone—a good distance away. There's a grunting sound and then I hear Tommy laugh.

"I got you, Mason. And I'm pretty sure that means I'm the last man standing."

Not for long.

I place my finger on the trigger of my gun. I watch as Tommy sort of rolls himself up, then plummets down into the scrubby bushes at the bottom of the tree. As soon as he's standing up, now busy brushing cockleburs off his legs with gloved hands, I move and take aim.

The red paint splatters over his chest and stomach like a weird art project. He looks down at his body, then up in my direction, his face frozen in shock. Carefully, I place my gun on the ground and unbuckle my helmet, letting my hair tumble down over my shoulders.

"M-Marijke?" Tommy chokes out. I smile and shrug.

"I got your text," I say, leaning down to pick up my gun again. Tommy is still staring at me and now Mason has moved to join him.

"So you came here . . . to go paintballing?" Tommy still looks shocked, but it's starting to morph into confusion. I shrug again.

"I wanted to see what all the fuss was about. You always say how fun it is. I figured I could use some fun—not to mention I got to take you down in the process."

He blinks at me, then looks over at Mason.

"Did you know about this?"

Mason throws up his hands.

"Naw, man, this is news to me."

I shrug and Tommy just shakes his head, watching me with astonishment on his face. He turns to Mason again.

"Dude, you want to go find Jimmy and Brendan?"

Mason nods, then looks at me again and grins. "By the way, that's the only time anyone's hit Tommy first. You should be proud."

"I think I am," I say, smiling back.

When Mason has disappeared through the trees, Tommy starts walking closer to me. He unbuckles his helmet as he goes and tosses it on the ground. He stops a few feet in front of me, and for a moment we just stand there, staring at each other. Then, hardly a second later, his mouth is on mine.

Tommy is kissing me in a way I haven't felt in a long time. If ever. He holds my face like I'm something precious, then moves his hands to my waist and pulls me even closer.

"Have I told you lately how amazing you are?" he whispers gruffly. I lean back to meet his gaze.

"You aren't mad?"

"Are you kidding? First of all, I've never been so shocked in my life, but more than that"—he rakes a hand through his hair and grins—"more than that, you have never looked so sexy in *your* life. And in coveralls, no less."

I look down at my fully covered body, then back up, giving him a shy smile.

"I drove an ATV up here all by myself too."

Tommy sort of groans and pulls me into his arms.

"You are like no one I've ever met, Marijke Monti. You know that's what made me fall for you in the first place."

I blink at him and open my mouth. It's the closest he's ever come to saying he loves me—that he's *fallen for me* pretty much means the same thing, right?

"I have a question for you," Tommy says.

Unable to respond, I just look up at him. His eyes are full of so much affection. I guess I really shouldn't be surprised about what happens next.

"Will you go to prom with me?"

In the movies when moments like this happen, time stands still. I mean, literally. The camera pans around the couple in a circle, catching every expression. My smile turns from happy to goofy and I don't even care. I wrap my arms around Tommy's neck and plant a kiss on his mouth.

"I would absolutely love to go to prom with you," I whisper against his lips. He pulls back to look at me.

"Are you disappointed?"

"In what?"

"In this. I know you were hoping for a billboard or skywriting or a hot air balloon."

I shake my head. "No, it's perfect. I couldn't have planned it better myself."

"Come on," Tommy says, slinging an arm over my shoulders. "It's time for our post-paintball ritual: omelets at the diner. Are you in?"

"You sure you don't mind if I crash your guy gathering?" I ask.

He squeezes me against him and kisses the top of my head. "Baby, I love that you're here right now."

"Good," I say, smiling up at him. "Because there's nowhere I'd rather be."

TWENTY-EIGHT

⇒ LILY ⇐

After dropping Marijke off at the paintball course, I head back to school, determined to get through some of those Senior Wills. I need to get as many typed up as possible, considering I've committed to sell raffle tickets after school next Monday. It'll make my time a lot more limited, and we're on a pretty tight deadline.

But as I pull into the upper lot, I notice the motocross track down below; a dozen or so riders are still circling it at what looks to be breakneck speeds. I think again about Olive Penderghast and her *Easy A* persona. She used clothes to send a message and then ended up finding the guy of her dreams.

If I've already found the guy, then I should be one step closer than she was, right?

I back out of my space and drive down the steep gravel

lane to the motocross track. There's a line of cars along one side; I slide in next to a Camaro and cut the engine.

"Okay, Lil, what's the plan?" I ask myself aloud. It's not like I could just walk onto the track and wave down Joe just to say hello. No, I need to have a reason.

I rack my brain and decide on debriefing him about this morning's SGA meeting. Then he'll know I'm spreading the word.

Sure, it's a flimsy cover, but it's better than, "Hey. Like my skirt?"

I unlatch the gate and move toward a set of old bleachers that are set up for people to watch the races. I climb up onto the first bench and smooth my skirt over my legs before I sit down.

The noise around me is almost deafening. The revving of one engine would be loud enough, but there are at least ten bikes on the track and a few more on the sidelines. Everyone seems determined to make the loudest growl their bike can muster. Maybe it's a guy thing. Or maybe that's just what a bike does to you—forces you to make noise like an animal just for the thrill of it.

I watch as a few riders direct their bikes up and over the bumpy inclines before dipping down into a fairly steep-sided ditch. That's when I notice Joe standing at one side of the track. He isn't suited up; in fact, he doesn't even have a bike with him. Instead, he's standing with another guy, his arms crossed over his chest. I can't help but admire how his tan arms contrast with his bright-blue T-shirt.

I wait until he moves toward the entrance to the track before scrambling back up and heading down the stairs. When I see him standing at the fence, I realize that the guy he's talking to isn't just anyone—it's his uncle Bobby, the X Games competitor. The one who is helping him sponsor the fund-raiser. Joe swings the gate open, and Bobby gives him a quick one-armed hug before walking back out to the parking lot. He turns to leave, so I force myself to call out to him.

"That's your uncle, right?"

Joe spins around and sees me standing there. His eyes turn wide and surprised, then he blinks rapidly, as if he's trying to control his reaction. Nervously, I reach up to touch my hair, making sure my curls are still tucked into place.

"Lily. Wow, I . . . what are you doing here?"

"I just wanted to let you know that I met with SGA this morning and everyone is totally into the idea of a raffle for the prom proposal. I told them we'd sell tickets on Monday after school—I mean, if that works for you, obviously."

"No, no, that's great," he says, shaking his head. "Thanks for taking care of that."

"It's not a problem. Oh, and we still have a roll of tickets from the winter fund-raiser, so I can grab those on Monday too."

Joe grins down at me. "You are amazing. How do you stay so organized?"

"It's just the way I'm put together, I guess."

His grin downgrades into that sexy, close-lipped smile of his.

"Speaking of put together . . . that's, um, some outfit you're wearing."

I can't believe it—I actually feel myself blushing.

So. LAME.

"It was Marijke's idea," I say, shrugging. "She thought I should spruce up my wardrobe a bit."

"Well, remind me to tell Marijke thank you."

Now I'm the one with wide eyes. I can't believe he just said that. He must realize I'm speechless, because he gives me a wink and takes a step backward.

"I gotta run over and check Bryan's wheel mount," he says, jerking a thumb over his shoulder. Then he raises an eyebrow. "But I'll see you tomorrow, right?"

I swallow hard. "Sure. Tomorrow."

"Great. Later, Lily."

For a second I just stand there. Then, with little effort and even less willpower, I'm walking or running or floating toward my car, the smile on my face like a force of nature.

TWENTY-NINE

⇒ MARIJKE ⇐

The first thing I do when I get home is call Lily and tell her everything that happened.

"So then what?" she asks.

"And then I had a western omelet. It was delicious."

She sighs. Even over the phone, I can hear the tinge of caution in her voice. She thinks I should have laid into Tommy. She thinks I didn't stick up for myself.

"Did you ask him why he didn't show up when he said he would?"

I shrug, even though she can't see me.

"He was supposed to go to the paintball arena yesterday, but a couple of the guys bailed. They rescheduled for after school today. He did text me, you know. I just didn't see it."

"I guess."

"Anyway," I say, trying to sound breezy, "you haven't heard the best part."

"And what's that?"

I take a deep breath, smiling at my reflection in my bedroom mirror.

"He asked me to prom."

Silence.

"Are you there?"

"Yeah," Lily says. "Sorry, I—I guess I'm surprised. How did he whip up a prom proposal so fast? I mean, he didn't even know you'd be there."

A tiny prickle of indignation starts to travel up my back. It heats my neck, then sets up shop in my cheeks, warming them to a rosy hue.

"It wasn't exactly a *proposal*. It was just a simple question. We were alone and having fun and he asked me. It was perfect."

"Oh."

I feel irritated. "Why, did you expect fireworks or something?" I snap.

"No," she says slowly. "But it isn't about what I expect. It's about what *you* expect—expect*ed*, anyway. And I thought you were really looking forward to a flashy proposal like everyone else."

"Well yeah, sure," I admit, "but when it came down to it, the flashy stuff just wasn't important. Not to mention that the only person providing the flash was me, what with my iPod-dock, flash-mobbing spectacles. And look how those worked out."

"I wouldn't say the incident in Tommy's yard was a spectacle, exactly."

"You know what I mean."

We're both silent for a second.

"So, do you want to go dress shopping with me tomorrow?" I finally ask her. "I found the cutest blue dress—the skirt is sort of puffy like a tutu. I can't wait to try it on."

Lily sighs. "I can't. I promised my mom I'd stick around the house and help with Mac."

"Okay. That's cool."

It feels strange to have this awkward distance between me and Lily.

"You looked killer today, by the way," I finally say. "The outfit was perfect. Did you get to see Joe?"

"Yep."

"And?"

"And I think he approved." Now I can hear a smile in her voice and I feel a little better. Then I hear a slam from beneath my floor. Then there's a muffled yell. I blink and pull the receiver away from my ear.

Is that my dad?

"Hey Lily, I gotta go."

We hang up and I run quickly from my room to the second-floor landing. Now I can hear my mom too.

"Damn it, Jeremy! You're so selfish, it's unbelievable."

I stop dead and blink at the stairs in front of me. I know my parents argue. I mean, everyone's parents have disagreements. But I have never heard them *yell* at each other. And my mother *never* curses.

Slowly, I start down the rest of the stairs. I hear Dad mumble something and Mom gives a sharp, humorless laugh.

"I can't believe you would say that to me," she hisses back at him.

I make it to the kitchen doorway and stare at them. Both of their backs are to me, but I can see the anger blooming from their postures. They are all edge, no curves.

"What are you guys fighting about?" I ask them.

At the sound of my voice, they both whip around to look at me. Dad's face is bright red and Mom is breathing hard. They look at each other cautiously, like they're making some sort of mutual decision.

"Hey sweetie—we, uh, didn't realize you were home yet . . ." The smile that spreads across my dad's face is as fake as it gets. I blink at him.

"Tommy dropped me off. I was upstairs on the phone. You didn't answer me—why are you guys fighting? You never yell at each other."

My mom shakes her head. Her hands are trembling and her lips are pressed together so hard, they look white.

"I can't do this right now," she mutters, now looking at

the floor. When she leaves the room and bounds up the stairs, I already know to prepare myself for a slamming door. Still, when it happens, I flinch. So does my dad.

"What is going on?" I demand, hands on my hips.

Dad shoots me a disapproving look. "Marijke. Watch the attitude."

I throw up my hands.

"Seriously, Dad? You and Mom were just screaming at each other, and you're worried about my attitude?"

He shakes his head. "I'm sorry. Your mother and I . . . we're just disagreeing about a few things. Don't worry about it, honey."

I narrow my eyes at him. His smile has disappeared, replaced with concern and stress that is stretched over his face. I've never seen him this unhappy. I don't know what to say to make him feel better.

"Okay, well, I'm going to go do my homework," I say, giving him a last look. Again, he flashes me a forced smile.

"Let me know if you need any help with calculus."

"Okay."

I walk back upstairs slowly, eyeing my parents' closed bedroom door. Dad said that everything is okay. But this time, I know he's hiding something. There's a pain in my chest I can't explain. Their perfect marriage can get irritating, sure—but this? I don't know who these people are and, worse, I don't think I want to.

Back in my room, I flop on my bed and stare up at the ceiling. I force myself to remember Tommy and prom, to remember I'm going dress shopping tomorrow. Practice picks back up next week and then states are on Friday. I have so much to look forward to, so I'm just going to look forward.

Besides, whatever is going on with my parents will blow over. I mean, even fairy tales have their ups and downs. Happily ever after just gets sidetracked sometimes.

THIRTY

⇒ LILY ⇐

I literally spend my whole weekend counting the seconds until Monday morning. I do this for two reasons. First, because Joe and I are selling tickets on Monday. I'm having this recurring daydream about our holding hands beneath a folding table in the student parking lot, then sneaking off to make out under the motocross bleachers.

It's a *really* great daydream.

And the second reason I wanted the weekend to end is my mom. Or, more specifically, my mom and Contractor Jim.

On Saturday, I woke up early, a little bitter that I wasn't going prom dress shopping with Marijke. I know this is the saddest thing ever, but I've never actually been clothes shopping with a friend. Even if I don't technically have a date to the dance, I really want to *get* a dress. It would have been fun to at least try them on—something a little sparkly, with a risqué slit up the side, or maybe something sort of lacy and romantic . . .

I snorted and shook my head.

Right. There's nothing like a sleek gown to make my mop of curls look all the more out of place. It's probably better I don't even let the fabric touch my body, thus enticing me into trying to be something I'm not.

Shooting down the vision of formal dresses, I padded downstairs and started getting our typical Saturday morning breakfast together—bacon, eggs, and peanut butter pancakes with sliced bananas. Over the years there have been a lot of changes, but Saturday morning breakfasts are a trademark Spencer tradition. When I was little, Mom had me on standby as she poured the batter into perfect circles. With the flick of a wrist, she'd pull up the ladle of batter, then point to me and I'd drop a few slices of banana into each pale puddle. When the pancakes came out, they were golden brown with a few little discs of caramelized banana embedded in each one.

It wasn't until the last year or two that I started making the pancakes myself. Once Mom saw I could handle the job, she started favoring sleeping in over motherly domesticity. It really didn't matter, actually. I love cooking for my family.

So, as I'm getting ingredients out of the fridge, there's a knock at the side door. I blink at it, then glance over at the clock. I can't imagine who would be here this early on a weekend.

When I open the door, I want to roll my eyes.

It's none other than Contractor "Your-Mom's-Too-Old-For-Me-Even-Though-I'm-Almost-Forty" Jim.

"Hey there, kiddo," he says, walking past me into the kitchen. "Something smells good."

Frozen, I stare at Jim as he plops down into a chair with his back to me, apparently oblivious to the fact that I'm still watching him.

Without a word, I set down the egg carton I'm still holding and march upstairs.

"Mom?"

I push her bedroom door open; it creaks loudly, but she isn't there. Then I notice her bathroom door is closed. I move quickly and knock on the door, a little harder than I need to.

"Mom?"

"Yeah baby?"

"Um, is there something you want to tell me?"

She pulls the door open and looks at me. Should I be surprised that she's putting on mascara and lip gloss this early?

"About what?" she asks.

"Um, about Jim coming over at the crack of dawn?" I cross my arms across my chest and glare at her.

"Oh, I invited him for breakfast," she says, shrugging.

"Mom, are you kidding me right now? Don't you remember what he said to you? *About* you?"

"Of course I do," she says, glancing in the mirror and fluffing her hair up around her shoulders, "but he apologized. Look, he brought me roses last night."

She gestures to her nightstand where a half-dozen red roses are wilting in a vase.

"He probably got them at the gas station," I mutter. Mom makes a tsking sound.

"Lily, just give him a chance, please."

"Mom, I *might* consider giving him a chance if he hadn't been completely horrible to you. But he *was* horrible—and I can't begin to understand why you can forgive him."

Mom puts a hand to her temple and rubs it lightly. "All right, Lily. Is there anything else I can do for you?"

Mom's tone is more honest than her facial expressions. I can tell she's getting annoyed.

"Yeah," I say. "You can make the pancakes yourself this time."

Mom smiles into the mirror again, pursing her lips into what I think is supposed to be a sexy pout. "Oh, that's a good idea, anyway. Jim hates bananas."

And so the weekend went, with Jim and my mom snuggling on the couch while my brother buried himself in video games and I buried myself in homework and movies. It's pretty sucky that "buried" is the verb I'm using here—as though *death* is the only analogy I can think of when I consider a weekend with my mom and her boyfriend. I guess I shouldn't be surprised that Mom let Contractor Jim off the hook; in the end, all he did was insult her and make her feel terrible about herself. She's forgiven guys for a lot worse than that. Heck, Mac's dad cheated on my mom more times than she probably even knows about, and she had *a kid* with him.

If anything good came out of my self-imposed isolation, it was my Drew Barrymore movie binge. Josie Grossie from *Never Been Kissed* is totally my inspiration this week.

So, as the sun rises on Monday morning, I'm out the door and down the driveway before my mom is even awake. Like Josie, I'm ready to confront the man I want to be with. I'm ready to prove to Joe Lombardi once and for all that I am the girl for him.

I clock-watch my way through my classes today, then book it to the lower parking lot at dismissal. Considering that there wasn't much time or talk about the fund-raiser, I'm blown away by the crowd of guys that are lining up by the cab of Joe's F-150 for the ticket sale. He's pulled down the gate and is sitting on it, chatting with the football team captain, Kevin Messner.

When Joe sees me coming, he grins. I resist the

temptation to turn around and make sure he's actually smiling at me.

While I didn't have the courage to rock the short skirt again today, I did choose a V-neck shirt with a little more cleavage than I'd normally be comfortable with and my jeans look decent, if a little tight. In one arm, I carry a metal cash box and, in the other, the stack of printed signs and a roll of raffle tickets.

"Quite the turnout," I say to Joe when I get closer. He nods enthusiastically.

"I know—amazing what flooding Twitter and Facebook with messages can accomplish." He glances at his phone. "Though we should probably do this quick in case the administration catches on. The last thing I need is another detention. Or worse."

"Yeah," I say, smiling up at him, "although it *would* give you time to get your precalc homework done."

"Ah, but only if you're there to help me."

I look down then, busying myself with the cash box. We're flirting—*he's* flirting—and it feels so natural. It's not my imagination, right? I think this is what people mean when they talk about chemistry—that feeling of push and pull so like gravity that it's a force in and of itself.

"Okay," Joe calls out over the crowd. "The Moto-Proposal raffle is open for business. Each ticket is five bucks and you can buy as many as you want. Give your money to Lily here and she'll give you a ticket and some directions for the drawing. Now, who's first?"

Joe really did come up with an amazing prom proposal. Honestly, it seems like the perfect proposal for *him* to do for someone. The motocross riders are going to ride their circuit and perform for the crowd, just like they're supposed to. But at a signal from Joe, they'll all line up at one end of the track and a vinyl banner saying WILL U GO 2 PROM W/ ME? will unfurl from one end of the line to the other. Then the proposer will come out onto the track wearing a full motocross getup. No one will know his identity until he takes off his helmet.

"And that's when the guy will grab the mic and officially ask the girl to prom," Joe is explaining to a senior I recognize from the track team.

"Sounds like there's gonna be a rack of people there, huh?" the guy asks. Joe nods.

"Well, any girl whose boyfriend hasn't asked her to prom yet is going to be there for sure," he says, counting a wad of one-dollar bills in his hand.

We sell more tickets than I could have imagined. I barely have time to breathe before a new guy is plunking down a five-dollar bill. About forty-five minutes later, Joe pops the gate back up and we sit on the uncomfortable metal truck bed counting the money in the cash box.

I double-check it to be sure, then look up at him, amazed.

"There's almost three hundred dollars here."

"Seriously?" Joe looks as blown away as I feel.

"Seriously." I grin at him. "That much cash in less than an hour? I think this really worked!"

"Yeah it did!" he says, letting out a whoop of excitement. He pulls himself closer to me and looks into my face, eyes shining. "Have I told you lately that you're a genius? This is definitely the best idea anyone's come up with."

Before I can respond, he leans over the cash box and wraps his arms around me in a tight hug.

"Thanks, Lily," he says in my ear. I shake my head, trying to control the smile that's beginning to take over my face.

"It's—it was fun. I'm glad it worked out."

As he pulls back, Joe pauses several inches from my face and I stop breathing. For a second, I think he might kiss me.

Like, *seriously*. He might actually kiss me.

But he doesn't. Instead he says, "Let's celebrate—wanna get a milk shake?"

There's only one answer to that question.

"Of course."

THIRTY-ONE

⇒ MARIJKE ⇐

"I can't believe I didn't find *anything* I liked on Saturday," I complain, flipping through a magazine of prom dresses. "What did you say this store was called again?"

"CoCo's," my mom says, turning right onto the highway. "Apparently it only buys one of every dress so that no girl will have the same thing on. Pretty cool, right?"

I nod, looking out the passenger-side window. It was nice that Mom let me play hooky this morning—it's not something she normally does, especially when the excuse is shopping.

"Why are you going in late to work again?" I ask her. She shrugs.

"You didn't find a dress this weekend and prom's coming up soon. I figured it would be nice for the two of us to do this."

I watch her face as we pull into the parking lot of CoCo's Boutique. There's something wrong—I can just tell by her tone of voice and the little frown at the corner of her lips.

But it doesn't take long for me to forget about my mom's facial expressions in favor of the sequins and satin of the dresses inside CoCo's. A woman named Veronica helps me pull dress after dress from the racks, then follows me to the dressing room.

"Ooh, this champagne chiffon will look divine against your skin," she drawls. I grin and turn to Mom for her opinion, but she's staring at the screen of her phone, shaking her head.

"Mom?" I ask hesitantly. She looks up quickly, then back at her phone again.

"Sorry, honey—I've got to take this call. Just let me know when you find something and we can buy it, okay?"

"Uh, okay . . ."

So much for a mother-daughter shopping trip.

I finally decide on a pale-blue dress—the fabric has a sort of shiny look, like glitter's been woven through it. It sweeps over one shoulder and molds to my body, then falls in a soft skirt to the floor. I feel like Cinderella—literally, the Disney version who has that blue gown that the birds and mice make for her. Or is it the one the fairy godmother makes appear with her magic wand? Either way, I love it.

From the window outside, Mom gives me a thumbs-up—I guess that means she likes it too.

When Mom drops me at school before lunch, she takes off her sunglasses and bites her lip.

"Are you coming straight home after school?" she asks me.

"I have practice again this week, remember? But I'll be home after practice."

"Good." She nods, then puts her sunglasses back on. "Call if you need a ride, okay?"

"Sure." I grab my backpack. "Mom, is something wrong? You just seem . . . weird."

She shakes her head, looking forward. "We'll talk when you get home."

Great. I can only imagine what that means. I'm sure it's got something to do with the college acceptance letters I've been dutifully ignoring for the last month and a half. I'll have to start preparing myself for the responsibility lecture again.

After school, I find Tommy sitting outside the cafeteria at a picnic table, guffawing at something Jimmy is saying.

"Right, man," Tommy replies. "That's what you gotta do—leave them always wanting more."

Jimmy is laughing too, but his face sobers a bit when he sees me standing there.

"Hey Marijke."

I cock an eyebrow as Tommy turns around. When he sees that it's me, his face breaks into a huge grin.

"Hey baby! Long time, no see. Did you find a dress this morning?"

I cross my arms. "Maybe. Will I have a reason to wear it or will you just be leaving me wanting more?"

Tommy's smile downgrades a bit. "I wasn't talking about you and me. I was talking about Jimmy and the chick he met at Skinners last week."

I glance over at Tommy's friend, who is turning a vibrant shade of tomato.

"You snag yourself a girlfriend, Jimmy?"

He grins, then shrugs. "Maybe. Hopefully she'll be there this weekend when we play again."

"This weekend?" I turn to Tommy. "You're playing Skinners again this weekend?"

"Yeah—didn't I tell you that?"

"Uh, no . . ."

He shrugs. "It's not a big deal."

"What day?"

"Saturday."

I just stare at him for a second. "You do remember what Saturday is, right?"

Tommy runs a hand up my arm and back down. The goose bumps set up shop on my shoulder and travel all the way to my wrist.

"Of course I remember what Saturday is. This won't interfere at all with the state meet. We don't play until nine. States will be over long before that."

I nod warily. "Okay. Just remember that Salverton is at least an hour away."

Tommy waves a hand. "It's not a problem. Trust me."

Trust.

I think I'm starting to hate that word.

THIRTY-TWO

⇒ LILY ⇐

Jimmie's is a roadside stand that's known for hot-dog-eating contests and the best chocolate shakes around. Joe didn't even have to ask what flavor I wanted when we got there—the chocolate malted is the only kind of milk shake Jimmie's makes. And yes, they're *that* good.

"To great ideas," Joe says, bumping his Styrofoam cup against mine. I grin over at him as we pull out of the drive-through lane and back out onto the road.

"And to the prom," I add. "Without it, there's no way you would have raised so much for Bikes for Tykes."

"We—*we* raised so much money."

"Okay, *we*," I agree.

He nods and takes a long sip through his straw.

"They're just such a pain. God, I know how I felt about it—I couldn't *wait* until I got mine out of the way."

"Your *what* out of the way?" I ask, confused.

"My prom proposal. I felt like a total loser the entire time. At least she said yes, or I'd be really up the creek."

I open my mouth, then close it. The chill from the surface of my cup begins to transfer down my arm and I hold it hard enough that my fingers begin to dent the white foam.

Joe has a date for the prom.

Well, of course he does, moron. Prom's in two freaking weeks.

"I—uh—I didn't hear about that one," I stutter, fiddling with my straw. "Who did you ask?"

Joe stretches a long arm over the bench seat and leans back a bit. The brim of his cap is shading his eyes, so I can't really see his expression.

"Barbara Marconi. My proposal was *totally* lame too. I did a scavenger hunt thing in the park—she had to follow hints I wrote in chalk on the paths. Then she found me at the end holding a sign."

He shrugs.

"Not my most creative idea, but it worked out in the end."

Blinking, I put the straw of my drink to my lips, but I don't take another sip. The milk shake that was once so delicious suddenly tastes just like liquid chalk.

"That sounds nice," I say finally, because it *does* sound nice. To have Joe go out of his way to do anything like that for me sounds more than nice. It also sounds impossible.

"So, are you and Barbara dating?" I ask, trying to sound casual.

He cracks a grin. "Nah, I'm buddies with her brother, Matt. He told me she had a crush on me and she didn't have a date for prom. Their family just moved here last year and I know she doesn't know a lot of people. I felt like it was the right thing to do, you know?"

I consider my options. I could let this all go with a smile and not say anything. Or I could actually say how I feel. I try to consider my options.

What would Josie Geller do?

What would Olive Penderghast do?

What would sarcastic, witty, turned-over-a-new-leaf-and-wearing-skirts Lily Spencer do?

As Joe pulls into the school parking lot, I suck in a deep breath and then shift in my seat. Suddenly, it's like someone flips a switch in me. Or, more accurately, like someone presses play. I know I have to do this now, or I'll never do it at all. Especially now that I know that his prom date is just a favor to a friend.

"So, listen," I begin, already talking way too fast, "I was wondering if you wanted to go out sometime."

Joe glances over at me, eyebrows high on his forehead. "Out? You mean, like, on a date?"

I shrug, but I force myself to meet his gaze.

"Yeah. Like a date. Or something."

"Wow, Lily," he begins. "I—uh—I don't know what to say."

He blinks a few times, then shakes his head. "You know you are totally great. I've had a blast hanging out with you over the last week. But—"

But.

But.

Who knew a word could actually cause physical pain? Out of self-preservation, I grab the handle and heave the heavy truck door open.

"Never mind. Just forget it," I manage to mumble. I start to slide out when Joe grabs my arm gently.

"No, wait. Seriously, I think you are totally awesome and you've been such a great help and everything . . ."

He trails off and I feel an inexplicable shot of fury blaze through me. I don't know who I'm angry at. Probably myself.

Joe scrubs a hand over his face, the other hand still on my wrist. He pulls his hat off and his dark hair is a little matted. Still, I swear he could model razors or deodorant or something equally as masculine.

"I just feel like—I mean, there's so much going on right now," Joe is saying, "what with Bikes for Tykes and prom and graduation . . ."

He trails off again, and I swallow hard.

"I'm just not looking to start anything serious," he says,

his voice low. "You are an amazing girl and any guy would be lucky to be with you . . ."

And I hear it—right away, I hear it. It's a tone impossible to mistake for anything but what it is.

It's pity.

He feels sorry for me.

I don't say anything else. I don't look at him. Instead, I grab my bag from the floor of the cab and slide back to the door.

"Wait," Joe says.

But I can't. I can't sit here and wait any longer.

"I gotta go," I mutter as I push open the door, then slam it shut behind me. I glance back at him like a reflex, but I can't see him through the glass. All I can see is my reflection. Just me, standing alone.

Somehow, it seems totally appropriate.

THIRTY-THREE

⇒ MARIJKE ⇐

As I pick up the broken pieces of my hand-built vase from the bottom of the kiln, I shoot Mr. Chastain, my art teacher, a guilty look. How is it that I'm always the one with projects that turn the kiln into a hazmat zone?

"I'm really sorry that this happened," I say for the fifteenth time. Mr. Chastain shakes his head.

"It's all right, Marijke. Just remember—you gotta wedge the clay really well before you start rolling it out."

I nod. I do know better, really. Rules of Clay 101 includes avoiding the air bubbles that can make your work blow up in the kiln. And since stuff only gets fired when the kiln is full, that means that my experiment in pyrotechnics ruined other people's hard work too. I wince at the shattered bowl Becca Prince made on the potter's wheel last week. It's bad enough when you screw up something of your own—but when you ruin something that doesn't even belong to you? Well, then you feel like Jerk of the Year.

I've just finished sweeping out the last of my vase's shattered bits when my phone vibrates in my pocket. I glance at the clock on the wall. I really need to head down to the track. Two-a-days start tomorrow and they'll continue up until Friday—the day before states. Four long days of double practices and high-protein meals. It's days like this where the word "jock" hits a little too close to home, kicking me right in my self-conscious butt.

I don't even bother looking at the phone's screen when I answer the call.

"I know, I know, I'm on my way," I say into the receiver.

"I never should have done this."

I blink then pull the phone back to look at the caller ID.

"Lily?" I ask, pressing the phone back to my ear. She doesn't say anything. I listen closely, covering my other ear. Then I hear a sniffle.

"Lily, are you *crying*?"

In the past few weeks, I've learned a lot about Lily. She is logical. She thinks. She makes plans. She doesn't freak out or overreact.

Basically, she's not like me.

Which makes her crying into the phone a completely foreign concept. There's only one thing that could make her this upset.

"Did something happen with Joe?" I ask. Lily sighs loudly.

"Yes. No. I don't know."

"Hold on a second." I grab my bag off the table and wave to Mr. Chastain. When I'm out the door, I take a deep breath.

"You guys were supposed to sell tickets today, right? How did that go?" I prompt her.

Silence. I wait another few seconds, then exhale hard.

"Lily, what is it? Did something happen? Tell me."

She makes a weird, defeated sound, a sort of groan mixed with a grunt.

"I asked him out," she finally says. "I asked Joe out, and he said no."

I stop at the locker room door and stare at it, trying to think of what to say.

"Wow—I didn't realize you were planning on doing that."

"Yeah, well. I saw my window and I took it."

When I get inside the locker room, I throw my bag on the floor and sit a on a bench. Already, the wheels in my head are spinning.

"You know," I say to Lily, "they say the best way to get over someone is to find someone else."

"Um, seriously?"

I shake my head, even though she can't see me. "Well, you've had this crush on Joe forever and maybe it's time you give someone else a chance."

She doesn't say anything; I take it as a signal to continue.

"You know, Tommy's bandmates are all single. Why don't I try to see if they want to hang out with us this weekend? We could try a double date . . . oh! Oh! Listen, it could be like in *The Notebook*—remember when Allie and Noah get set up on that movie date and they fall in love and all?"

For a second, I can't hear anything. I pull the phone from my ear to check if I have service when I hear her speak again. She doesn't sound happy.

"Please tell me you're kidding."

"What's the problem?" I ask her. "Mason's supercute, right? And Jimmy—I mean, he isn't a rocket scientist or anything, but that doesn't mean—"

"Marijke. I am *in love* with Joe Lombardi. *Just* Joe Lombardi. I've been *in love* with *just* Joe Lombardi for the last two years. I don't want a replacement. *I want Joe.*"

"Exactly. Come on—focus. Think about the movies. Remember *Drive Me Crazy*? It's all about how you can use one person to get the person you really love. Of course, then the two users fall for each other in the end . . . but it's a movie, so that's what you expect to happen."

"That's disgusting."

"Well, jealousy is one way to get a guy and it usually works. Maybe you need to embrace your devious side."

"Just forget it," she snaps. "Like I said, I never should have done this. There's a reason all these things work in movies. It's because they're fiction."

"Come on, Lily, don't give up . . ."

"No. I should have known better than this. I don't know why I thought this could actually work out."

She sounds broken. She sounds completely unlike the funny, snarky girl I've come to know.

"I was so sure this would change everything," she whispers, "and maybe it will for you, Marijke. Maybe the movies are the key to *your* happily ever after. But they aren't the key to mine. And I don't know why I let myself believe I was different."

"You *are* different," I say. "Come on, look at you. You've totally put yourself out there. Volunteering to help with Bikes for Tykes, wearing that sexy outfit—think about it!"

She scoffs into the phone, and suddenly her usual sarcasm is back in full force.

"Yeah, for all the good that did me. And you know what? That I can thank *you* for—thank you *so very much* for forcing me to be someone I'm not."

I blink rapidly. "I-I never meant to change you—that wasn't the point."

"Yes, it was—you *know* it was. Because you knew the truth—that Joe would never have been attracted to me just as I am. Or was. Or whatever."

For a second, we both sit in silence, letting her accusations and anger and my confusion and hurt simmer and condense around us. Finally, she sighs.

"Look, I just wanted you to know that I'm calling it off."

"Calling what off?"

"This—whatever this stupid plan was. I'm done. I've reached my conclusion and there's no reason to keep trying all these crazy schemes. It's over for me. So you're off the hook."

"What are you talking about?"

"You're off the hook. You don't have to pretend to be my friend anymore."

I jerk back, almost toppling over the bench.

"Seriously? You think I'm *pretending* to be your friend?"

"Well, aren't you?"

I'm a little surprised at the tears that prick the corners of my eyes. I mean, all my emotion has been tied up with Tommy and the movie plans Lily and I have come up with. But truthfully, I've been spending more time with Lily than I have with Tommy or my teammates or anyone else for that matter. And I've had more fun with her than I've had in a long time.

They say you can fall in love at first sight. What about falling into friendship? Can you become BFFs over the course of a few short weeks?

"If that's what you think, then I guess there's no reason for us to keep talking," I say, unable to hide the bitterness in my voice. "I thought—I thought I could really trust you. I thought we were . . ."

I trail off, shaking my head.

"Whatever. I've got to get out on the track. I'm missing practice."

I wait for a response, but there's nothing but a short buzzing noise, then empty space. I glance at the phone's screen. The call was disconnected. Either she hung up or something happened to the connection.

I guess it doesn't really matter now anyway.

THIRTY-FOUR

⇒ LILY ⇐

I'm not really mad at Marijke. Well, I *am*—I'm just more mad at myself. For once in my life, I can't get home fast enough. I want to curl up under the covers and block out the world.

Despite my best efforts, Joe's face flashes through my mind again. The pity in his expression was completely obvious—and totally humiliating.

But it's not as if I should have expected anything different.

I don't know what I was thinking.

That's my new mantra.

Home doesn't prove to be any better, though. The second I walk in the door, I see Mom running through the kitchen half-dressed with the phone pressed against her ear.

"I said I was getting ready," she says into the receiver. Her voice is breathless and sort of scratchy.

"Mom, what's going on? Are you sick?"

I follow her out into the living room, but she waves a hand at me and shakes her head. Then she coughs.

"Jim, I heard you. I understand, I'll be ready in ten minutes."

She slaps the phone down on the coffee table and I stare at her.

"What was that?" I ask. She shakes her head.

"Nothing."

Mom starts up the stairs, but I'm not willing to let it go. I barrel after her.

"Was that Jim on the phone?"

No answer.

"Seriously? You're gonna let him talk to you like that?"

Sighing, she turns around on the top step and I jerk to a halt behind her. "He had a bad day, Lily. We're going to get some dinner and maybe go bowling."

"Mom, you're sick. You can't go to the smokiest building known to man if you have a cold."

"I'm fine—it's just allergies."

I cross my arms. "So I'm assuming I'm watching Mac then?"

Mom crosses her arms too. "Yes, I was going to ask if you wouldn't mind doing that."

"Oh really?" I hear the scorn dripping off my words. "Were you really going to ask me if I wouldn't mind? Or were you just going to take off and expect me to do it?"

She narrows her eyes. "I don't know what has gotten into you, young lady, but I didn't raise my daughter to talk back like this."

"That's because you hardly raised me at all," I mutter, pushing past her and stomping into my bedroom. I don't wait for her to respond before I slam my door.

I don't come out again until I'm sure she's gone. The sound of Jim's car pulling into the driveway, then the opening and closing of the front door signal that it's safe to come out. I pad out over the carpet and duck my head into Mac's room, where he's lying on his bed, staring at the little TV on his dresser.

"Hey buddy."

He glances up at me, then back at the screen.

"Hey."

"You all right? Want me to make something to eat?"

"Nah. I'm okay."

I sit on the edge of his bed. "Are you upset about Mom leaving?"

He shrugs.

"She said she was going to make macaroni and cheese for me—the good kind, with the shells. I guess she forgot."

I reach over and give his shoulder a light punch.

"You saying I can't make the good kind of macaroni and cheese? Are you questioning my kitchen prowess?"

Mac wrinkles his nose. "What's prowess?"

"Don't worry about it." I heave myself back up. "I'll call you when it's ready, okay?"

"Okay. Thanks, Lily."

I give my brother a smile and try to pretend his sadness doesn't make me even more angry at my mom.

"No problem, little dude."

A half hour later, I'm willing to admit Mac is right—the macaroni and cheese with the shells is *so* much better than that other powdery box stuff. I groan in satisfaction as I take another bite. This is exactly what I needed to drown my sorrows in.

I camp out on the sofa and channel surf until I land on *Mean Girls*. Regina George has just pretended to like some girl's skirt, then made fun of it behind her back. Seeing that makes me wince.

Why did I think I could break into a crowd that I never belonged to?

Why did I try so hard to fit in when it was so freaking pointless?

I think the worst part, though, is that I know Marijke isn't like Regina George—at least not when it comes to being a queen bee who wants to rule the school. She was actually becoming a good friend. In the end, it doesn't really

matter. Just like in the movies, the silly, unpopular girl realizes that what she wanted in the beginning isn't nearly as
important as she thought.

I guess my life is like the movies after all—just not in a
good way.

THIRTY-FIVE

⇒ MARIJKE ⇐

"Marijke, hang back for a second."

Coach Mason has a couple of different voices—this is the one he uses when he's about to ream someone out. Great.

Yeah, it wasn't my best practice. I know that. I can't help that Lily's phone call is still echoing in my head. Had I forced her into being someone she wasn't? Had I just been using her to get my ideas to work? Really, neither of us had succeeded—there isn't an "I love you" in my life yet, and Joe is out of Lily's reach.

"Marijke," Coach says again, his voice filled with undisguised disappointment.

"Yeah?"

I slow my pace and wait for him to rip into me. Instead, he falls into step beside me and gives me an uncharacteristic look of concern.

"Is everything all right with you? I've never seen you so . . . so disconnected from your body. I don't think you even recognized the hurdles were there today."

I shake my head. "I didn't get to warm up. I was late because I had to clean up the kiln in the art room. There was an accident . . . don't even ask. I'm sorry. It won't happen again."

"Well, okay . . ." Coach Mason clutches a baton in one hand. Then he reaches out and gives my shoulder a light, encouraging pat. I rear back and stare at him. It's the first time he's ever made physical contact in the four years I've been running for him.

"I'm worried about you," he says, looking me in the eye. "Don't push yourself so hard that you can't find a reason to love this sport anymore."

"I, uh—"

I'm totally speechless. Coach just smiles and falls back to talk to Marcie, our discus thrower.

He's right, you know, a voice says in my head. *Obsessing about things makes you crazy.*

I brush off that voice, which is usually wrong anyway. I mean, she's the one who says that Tommy is cheating and ends up making me look like a possessive freak. And she's the one who thinks Tommy's lying when he says he's at band practice or out with his family. It's *her* fault we fight all the time. It's *her* fault I can't accept things as they are.

Not to mention she's the one who tells me Tommy doesn't love me after all.

I throw my shoulders back and try to put some purpose in my step. Lily's phone call knocked me off my game, but I can't let anything get in my way of winning the state competition.

Focus. That's what I need to do.

I need to focus on running fast and loving Tommy and prom and graduation. I need to focus on the future.

Still, when Beth drops me off at home after practice, I stand in the driveway and stare at the front door for a good minute. The last thing I feel like doing right now is facing my parents. Unfortunately, when I come through the front door, I've got a full view of Mom and Dad sitting in the living room. I force myself not to roll my eyes. Instead, I plaster a smile across my face and move into the room, flopping down into a recliner.

"What's up, guys?" I ask them. "What's for dinner?"

"Uh, Marijke," Dad begins, running a hand over his face, "your mom and I—we needed to talk to you. About something important."

Great. I'd forgotten about this.

Since I already know what this is about, I attempt to head them off.

"I know what you're going to say—you're pissed that I haven't chosen a college yet. And I get it, I do. I'm just trying to be thorough and really think things through."

But Mom's shaking her head. Her eyes look a little watery.

"No, honey. It's not that." She takes a deep breath and looks over at Dad, then back at me. "Your father and I have decided to take some time apart."

I blink at her, confused. "Time apart from what?"

My dad sucks in a breath and I turn to look at him. The pain on his face is evident. "Time apart from each other, sweetie. I'm going to be staying in a hotel for a while."

There are times when the world just doesn't make sense—like those videos where tiger cubs are cuddling with golden retrievers or where Vegas magicians manage to levitate in the middle of a crowd in front of the Bellagio hotel. It's like the laws of nature cease to exist.

And right now, in this room, that's exactly how I feel.

"What are you talking about?" I finally manage to say, looking from my mom to my dad and back again. "I mean, you guys are so happy. You hardly ever fight. You come to all my meets, you support me—you're great parents."

"And we'll continue to be great parents," Mom says, attempting a soothing tone. "Your father and I . . . well, it's just time for us to get some space. To find some perspective."

Dad sort of snorts at that. Mom shoots him a dirty look.

"Do you have a better rationalization?" she asks him icily.

"Marijke's practically a grown-up, Mary Ann. She doesn't need coddling. She needs straight answers."

"Oh, and you have those answers, I suppose? Please, lay one on me."

Dad rolls his eyes. "This is what I'm talking about with you—the constant sarcasm."

He storms out of the room, and Mom gets up and moves toward the fireplace. She puts her arm on the mantel and brushes the tips of her fingers along the edge of a silver frame. It's a picture of the three of us at a backyard barbecue. For a second, we both stare at that picture as if it's a reverse mirror. It's showing us the opposite of everything we are at this moment.

"Your dad and I were really young when we got married," Mom says.

"So?"

"So," she sighs, "I think that sometimes when you get married young, you don't have a chance to fulfill all the dreams you had growing up. Your dad always wanted to travel, and I thought about going to college more than once. But we never did those things."

I blink at her and she shrugs.

"We've been together twenty years, but for the first time it feels like we're holding each other back rather than pushing each other forward."

"You can live your dreams and be together."

Mom shakes her head again. "I know this is hard to understand, honey. We've given it a lot of thought, and I think that it's time we tried a life apart to see if we can be happier than we are together."

"Are you getting a divorce?"

The question hangs in the air. Mom won't meet my gaze.

Slowly, I move to standing and walk toward the stairs. Now, I notice the set of matching luggage stacked in one corner of the family room. Dad's luggage—the stuff he takes on business trips or vacations. They'd timed this presentation perfectly, I guess. Waited for me to get home from practice, planned to try and make it relatively painless.

Dad walks back in from the kitchen, his eyes a little red.

"Marijke," he says, "please, we need to finish discussing this."

I turn around and glare at him, shaking my head until I can hardly see clearly.

"I can't believe you'd just give up like this," I practically spit. Then I turn to look at my mom. "And I can't believe you'd let him. Love, *real* love—it's worth fighting for, you know? It's worth doing *everything* you can to save it. Even if it means making a fool of yourself. Even if it means losing the person you love in the end. As long as you've really tried— well, then you know that you've done all you can."

I whirl around and hurry toward the stairs.

Once I get to the second floor, I fly into my room and slam the door as hard as I can. On one side of the wall, the impact sends a tremor through everything that's hanging there, including a variety of track medals. I move to grab them and, with a sort of wail, yank them down off their places of glory.

I flop facedown on my bed and stare at the pattern on my comforter. I can't believe this is happening. My dad is moving out? Just like that? I blink back the tears, but unlike earlier, I can't keep these ones at bay. The sobs begin to wrack my body like a tide that's pulling me under. I've forgotten how to tread water. I've forgotten how to breathe. I need someone to tell me it's going to be okay. I need someone to reassure me and hug me and hold me.

I need Tommy.

I try his cell, but he doesn't answer. I send him a text and wait a few minutes until he responds:

Tommy: Hey baby, whattup?

Me: Can u come over?

Tommy: Now?

Me: Yeah, now. I need 2 talk 2 u about something important.

Tommy: Is everything OK?

Me: No. I'm all messed up. Just come, pls.

Me: I know it's short notice . . .

Tommy: Nah, it's fine. Give me like 30 min, alright?

Me: OK. Thanks.

Tommy: Sure, babe. Hang in till I get there.

✳ ✳ ✳

I don't know when I fell asleep, but when I wake again, it's morning. I sit up and look around. My alarm clock says 6:00 a.m. and the sun is just coming up. I push the snooze button and fall back against my pillows. I can't believe I slept almost twelve hours. I must have been exhausted.

And then it comes crashing back—the reality of yesterday. Lily's phone call. My terrible track practice. My parents' faces as they tell me that they're seperating.

I close my eyes. Maybe I can fall back asleep and pretend none of it ever happened.

Then I remember texting with Tommy. He was supposed to come over last night. Did I sleep through his visit? Had my parents sent him home?

Frowning, I grab my phone and slide my finger over the screen. There are no missed calls. There are no missed texts.

I move to the Facebook icon and click once. Scrolling down to Tommy's profile, I scan his last status update.

Just finished up the perfect practice. Falling into
bed and dreaming of guitar chords.

12:35 a.m.

He didn't call. He didn't text. And he didn't even bother showing up, even after I'd told him I was a mess. Even after I'd practically begged.

What else do you need to see?

The voice in my head is right this time, isn't she? What else *do I* need to see? What other evidence do I need?

Tommy's always been my number one priority. I've put off making choices about my future because I so desperately wanted to be with him. Yet when I ask him to be here, he flakes.

My mom's words from last night come rushing back.

We've been together twenty years, but for the first time it feels like we're holding each other back rather than pushing each other forward.

I swallow, blinking back hot tears.

I can't believe I got it so wrong. I thought it would be *so easy* to get Tommy to fall in love with me. But I forgot the most important part—the part that Lily understood when Joe rejected her and the part my parents understand too, since my dad is moving out.

Falling in love means two, not one. You can't get someone to love you through sheer effort or desire—not unless that effort or desire is mutual.

And it's not. You know that now, don't you?

"Yes."

I say it to my empty bedroom, but it doesn't make it hurt any less.

A breakup is something physical. I never understood this until I felt my own coming at me like a freight train. The breakup of my new friendship with Lily, the breakup of my parents' marriage, and now the breakup of my relationship with Tommy. All of them combined into one speeding vehicle, ready to blast through my body and leave my heart a twisted, mangled mess.

That's when I realized why they call it a breakup—it isn't just the way it leaves your relationships in tatters. It's also about the way it tears your heart into pieces, the way it makes you ache from the inside out.

PART THREE

AND . . . ACTION!

THIRTY-SIX

> LILY <

For the rest of the week, I manage to disappear—or, at least, I manage not to be seen.

It sure wasn't easy. I've gotten used to meeting up with Marijke in the morning or at lunch. I've become accustomed to walking by Joe's locker during the day. Now I've had to switch up my routine to avoid these two people. It sort of reminds me of the plug-in GPS my mom keeps for road trips and the mechanical voice declaring that it's "recalculating the route" when we've made a wrong turn.

My route recalculation involves a couple of strategic moves, but I manage to keep it going. The library turns out to be my salvation, which I guess isn't that surprising. I spend mornings before school and every lunch sitting at the same round table in the back corner, partially hidden by a shelf of obsolete *National Geographic* magazines.

By Friday, I've managed to adjust to a new version of my daily routine. It feels less like hiding and more like reliving my past. I try not to think about that—about how things were before when I was invisible. If I'm being honest, I know that it felt good to be a part of something, even if that something was a failed plan at finding love. If I'm being even more honest, I really miss Marijke.

But I really don't feel like being honest with anyone, especially myself.

So school has become uncomfortable for sure, but home has become downright unbearable. Apparently, Contractor Jim has decided to take up semipermanent residence in our house. I guess Mom isn't worried about the impression she's making on Mac anymore. He doesn't really seem to mind, considering he's gotten a handful of new DS games over the past week. Jim sure knows his bribery—at least when it comes to the boy sector of the population.

I, on the other hand, have been inexplicably graced with a gift set of sickly sweet body products that make me smell like a stripper. Not surprisingly, Mom loves them.

On Friday, though, I do something I've never done before—I play hooky.

"Mom, I just don't feel well," I complain, burrowing into my comforter and closing my eyes. "I need to take a mental health day. Get myself feeling better. I've just been working too hard."

Mom lays the back of her hand against my forehead. It feels cool. Huh. Maybe I actually *do* have a fever . . .

"All right. Well, you have been working hard, I'll give you that much." She glances at the clock on my night table, then moves to stand up. "I've got to head to work. And I'll be home late tonight—Jim's taking me back to Skinners. Mac's at the Burgees' house for the Boy Scout retreat."

"Sure."

I roll away to face the wall and I guess she takes that as a signal to go. I feel her hover over me, then plant a swift kiss on my hair. Part of me wants to wince at the sign of affection. Another part of me feels like crying.

I don't go back to sleep. Instead, I wait until the house is empty, then I get up and work on cleaning up the house. Since having Jim as a houseguest, my mom has let domestic chores fall to the wayside. Shocker.

The pile of pizza boxes by the recycling bin are evidence of our unvaried meal plan over the past week, and the sinkful of dishes is further proof of her neglect. It's so typical. Every time Mom falls in love, the housework is the first thing to be forgotten.

So I clean the house, I work on my history project, and I do everything I can not to think about Joe. The Bikes for Tykes event is tonight. Just knowing I won't be there makes the physical ache in my chest return with a vengeance. Then again, I guess this is how things work when I get involved.

The SGA activities always end up the same way—I never get any credit and people don't even remember I was part of the planning.

I used to be able to see the bright side of working behind the scenes. Now, somehow, I just feel bitter.

I sit at the computer and pull up the flyer I created for the raffle ticket sales. Looking at it, I remember Joe's enthusiasm—how he'd been so pleased by my efforts. The way his eyes crinkled, the way his lips curled into a smile when he would look at me.

This is clearly *not* a distraction.

I glance at the clock—it's not even lunchtime. I swallow hard and look back at the computer screen. I can't keep sitting here staring at everything I'm missing, despite all my best efforts not to. I need to go lose myself in something. I need to find an escape that will shut out everything I'm trying so hard to forget.

THIRTY-SEVEN

⇒ MARIJKE ⇐

The old movie theater looks different to me this time. Less charming, more . . . dilapidated. The bricks have that slightly crumbling look to them, and the cracks in the sidewalk are the kind that spiderweb across their width and allow weeds to sprout up in the broken places.

As I walk toward the front of the building, I feel another surge of heartbreak. I force myself not to think about Tommy, not to think about my parents. I just want to lose myself in a movie and forget where I am.

When Harry Met Sally . . . is playing this week. It might be considered a movie that someone my age can't relate to, but I totally disagree. It's about two people who prove the ultimate lesson in love—that you need to know someone inside and out before you fall in love with him. It doesn't matter how old you are; it's a fact that applies to everyone.

There's a good twenty minutes until the show starts, so I head over to The Coffee Grind for something frothy and delicious, preferably with a mound of whipped cream on top. Why not spoil myself today? A jolt of caffeine combined with a sugar rush could only be an improvement to my bummed-out behavior over the past week.

There's a line of people at the counter, so I move to the end and peer up at the specials board. Out of the corner of my eye, I see a girl with a dark curly ponytail sitting in the same seats Lily and I chose when we were here. God, I can't believe that was less than a month ago. Somehow it feels like it's been years. Or like it happened yesterday. How is that possible?

Inexplicably, the girl turns to look at me. When our eyes meet, hers widen. I think mine do too.

"Lily?"

She blinks at me, then she's up out of her seat and heading for the door. I spin on my heel and hurry after her. She ignores me when I call her name.

"Lily, stop!"

She seems to underestimate the fact that I'm a runner and even faster without any hurdles in my way. Finally, she slows down to a stop, but she doesn't turn to face me.

"Hey," I say, a little breathless. I come around to stand in front of her.

"Hey."

She meets my gaze head-on.

"What are you doing here?" she asks, her confusion obvious. "Why aren't you at school?"

I shrug. "I, uh . . . I just couldn't hack it today."

"You cut school?"

"Something like that."

"Yeah, me too." She shoves her hands in her pockets.

"Wow." I step back, impressed. "I guess there's a first time for everything. So what are *you* doing here?"

Lily toys with her necklace and looks past me toward the theater. "I just wanted to be distracted from moping and being a generally miserable human being. A movie seemed like a good bet."

I snort a laugh of disbelief. "I was thinking the same thing."

She smiles now for the first time. "Pretty crazy that we'd both end up here again."

"Yeah, pretty crazy," I echo.

She cocks her head and examines my face. I know what she's looking at—my eyes are red and there are dark shadows beneath them. I'm not wearing any makeup and the oversize sweatshirt I'm wearing has some sort of stain on the front—chocolate maybe. I didn't even notice it when I put it on.

"Is everything okay?" she asks, peering at me. "You look like . . . well, a hot mess, frankly."

I give her a rueful smile.

"Not really," I say. "I—Tommy and I broke up."

She stares at me, eyes wide. "Seriously?"

"Yeah. On Monday my parents told me they were splitting up, and when I asked Tommy to come over—"

"Wait." She holds up a hand. "What do you mean your parents are splitting up?"

I shrug. "They said they needed time apart. My dad moved to a hotel. I haven't seen him since Tuesday."

"Jesus, Marijke. I'm so sorry."

I give another shrug. "So when I asked Tommy to come over after my parents told me the news, he totally bailed. I've been avoiding him ever since."

"So you didn't actually *break up*, break up?"

"I wrote him a letter and gave it to him on Tuesday. It said everything I needed to say. I was too afraid I'd chicken out if I actually had to say what I wanted to say face-to-face."

We stand there for a second, just looking at each other. Lily's expression has softened a little since I first saw her in the coffee shop.

"I'm so sorry," she says again. And then she steps forward and folds me into a hug.

"I feel like we did all this work for nothing." I sigh. She pulls back and gives me a sad smile.

"Yeah. I feel like that too."

"But Lily, listen—I know that you think I was just using

you to get what I wanted from Tommy, but, seriously, that wasn't it. And I really miss you. You've—you've become a really great friend to me."

She and I have both lost more than we expected to when we started this whole experiment. The least we could do is gain one another.

As if reading my mind, she links her arm through mine.

"Come on. Let's go watch *When Harry Met Sally* . . . and eat our weight in junk food."

"You sure you want to go to the movies with me? I have a reputation for falling to pieces and crying my eyes out."

She shrugs. "Eh, I've got tissues. And besides, this movie is more about friendship than it is about love."

I look up at the scrolling sign above the theater doors. AND THEY ALL LIVED HAPPILY EVER AFTER rolls across the screen. I look at Lily, then motion up.

"You still believe in that?"

"In what? Happily ever after?"

"Yeah."

She shrugs. "I don't know about 'ever after.' But I do believe in 'happily.' "

"Yeah," I say, smiling at her. "So do I."

THIRTY-EIGHT

⇒ LILY ⇐

Somehow, sitting in the movie theater, I feel more at home than I've felt in a long time. Maybe it's because it seems like Marijke and I have come to a conclusion we can both respect—that the movies didn't bring us love, but they did bring us friendship. That the movies aren't a solution for problems, but they are a place to forget the problems you have. At least for a while.

As we chow down on a bucket of extra-buttery popcorn, I can't help but grin over at her. This isn't how I saw this day panning out, but like any good chick flick, the friends always win out in the end.

"*The Sisterhood of the Traveling Pants*," I whisper to her.

"Huh?" she whispers back.

I gesture between the two of us. "That's us. That's our movie—minus the pants."

"And minus the traveling and minus the sisters," Marijke points out. I roll my eyes.

"Thanks, Captain Obvious. You know what I mean."

She smiles at me and shakes her head. "I don't know if I would have acted out all those crazy movie scenes if I knew I'd be going on a movie date with *you* in the end."

I scoff, pretending to be offended, but I know what she means. And that niggling pain, the loneliness we both feel, becomes all the more obvious when Harry attempts to convince Sally that he loves her, that she's the person he wants to spend the rest of his life with.

When I glance over at Marijke, she doesn't even bother hiding her tears. Frankly, neither do I.

In the end, we'd both be lying if we said this is the way we envisioned our experiment ending. All the movies we've watched and studied and copied—well, they all had happy endings, despite potential outside variables. That's not how real life works, I guess. No director, no writer, no second or third or fourth takes. You get one shot to do it right the first time and, when it doesn't work, you have to live with the outcome.

After the movie ends, neither of us particularly feels like going home, so we head back over to The Coffee Grind. School is just letting out and Marijke thinks she has less of a chance of running into Tommy if she sticks around the theater, then heads back to school for practice.

"Isn't the Bikes for Tykes fund-raiser tonight?" she asks me. I shrug, then take another sip of my coffee.

"Yeah."

"Are you going?"

"Um, no, not a chance," I say. "After everything that happened with Joe—well, I just don't feel comfortable anymore."

She grimaces. "I really am sorry. It wasn't supposed to work out this way."

"It wasn't your fault. I chose to pursue Joe. I'm the one who put myself in the position to be rejected."

Marijke takes a long sip of her CocoLocoMocha and pokes the straw through the thick swirl of whipped cream.

"So now what?" she finally asks me. I shrug.

"Honestly, I think it's about time we call this thing quits. The movie experiment is officially a bust."

"Yeah. I guess you're right."

Marijke sighs and, on the table, her phone vibrates. She doesn't even bother looking at it.

"Is it him again?" I ask. She's the one who shrugs this time.

"Probably."

Apparently Tommy has texted her more than a dozen times a day since Tuesday—and that was only after he stopped calling and leaving multiple voice mails. She never checked them, so eventually her mailbox was full. Now he just keeps sending texts.

"I'm starting to regret getting that unlimited data plan on my phone," Marijke says.

"When did you give him the letter, anyway?" I ask.

"When he came to pick me up for school on Tuesday. He acted like nothing had happened, and I refused to speak during the entire drive to school. When we got there, I handed him the letter and walked away."

"Wow. What did it say?"

Marijke swallows a gulp of her drink. "It said that I'd given things a lot of thought and that I was sorry, but I just couldn't do it anymore. And then I told him about the movie experiment."

"You *what*?"

She shrugs again. "I just figured I might as well explain it. I mean, he pretty much missed out on everything I'd worked so hard to plan for him. He needed to know how hard I'd been willing to work to win his love."

I shake my head. "Did you tell him everything?"

"Yep. I even gave him a copy of that scientific method thing you typed up."

I toss my empty paper cup into a nearby trash can. "So now what? What about prom?"

Marijke winces. "I don't know. Honestly, I'm *so* tempted not to go, but I know it's the last prom I'll ever go to, so I sort of feel obligated. And I guess I kind of want to."

"I know what you mean," I say, nodding. "I don't want to

go stag, but I don't want it to seem like I think people can't go without a date. I just don't know if I can handle seeing Joe with a date."

"Whatever happened with that, by the way? You never gave me the full story." She leans over and rests her face in her cupped palm. I just shake my head.

"I asked him out; he said he didn't want anything serious right now."

"And?"

"And that any guy would be lucky to have me, blah, blah, blah. And 'but.' A big 'I like you, but.'"

Marijke sort of scoffs. "Well, come on, it's not like he *totally* rejected you, he said he didn't want something serious. Don't you get what that means?"

"Uh, yeah. It means he doesn't want to be with me. That he's blowing me off."

"No." She groans. "It means that he sees you as the kind of girl to get serious with, and he's not ready for that now."

I blink at her. "How could you possibly derive that out of what I just told you?"

"Because it's total guy language. He thinks you're a serious girl—the kind of girl to *get serious* about. He doesn't want to hurt you, and he's got other stuff going on."

"Huh. I never thought about it like that."

She rolls her eyes. "Obviously. How did you react when he said all of this to you?"

I wince. "I got out of his truck as fast as possible. And I've spent the week avoiding him. And avoiding you too."

"Yeah, I figured that one out on my own."

I drop my head into my hands. "I guess I should have considered the brighter side of his rejection—but really, it took every ounce of bravery I had to ask him out at all. Hearing him say no was about as painful as it gets."

Marijke takes another sip of her drink, then tosses it in the garbage.

"You want me to be honest with you, right? No BS?"

I nod and she leans a little closer.

"I think you caught him off guard. I think a guy like Joe is used to being the pursuer. He's the kind of guy that takes charge."

I sigh. "I guess. It's a little useless speculating about it now."

We lapse into silence and Marijke glances at her phone.

"Three new text messages," she murmurs. Taking a deep breath, she taps on the envelope icon and reads them. Then she hands the phone to me.

Tommy: Marijke, baby, pls. IDK what else I can say 2 u.

3:32 p.m.

Tommy: Let's meet up—I need 2 c u. I miss u.

3:37 p.m.

Tommy: If I have 2 stand in ur driveway all afternoon, I will.

3:42 p.m.

She sighs. This time I lean forward.

"So what are you going to do?"

"What do you mean?"

"I mean, he's not going to stop texting you or trying to get you back until you've talked to him again face-to-face. You need to tell him that you love him."

"*What?*" she looks dumbfounded. "Why in the world would I do that *now*?"

"Because then he'll understand."

"That doesn't make any sense."

I cock my head. "Maybe. Maybe not. But I know one thing—he's not going to let up until you've given him a chance to get closure. And besides, wouldn't you rather get that out of the way before the meet tomorrow? That way it isn't hanging over you while you race."

"You could be right," she admits. "But the last thing I'm going to do is hunt him down. I've spent enough time focused on Tommy. If he wants to talk to me that badly, he can find me himself."

THIRTY-NINE

⇒ MARIJKE ⇐

Ever heard the phrase "be careful what you wish for"?

I really should have paid closer attention to it.

As Lily turns onto my street, I see the General Qi before I see Tommy. Lily sees it too; she glances over at me with a nervous expression.

"You want me to stick around?" she asks. I shake my head.

"No. It's fine. I need to face him. It's like you said, it's better if I don't have it hanging over me at states."

"Okay," she says, sounding a little unsure. I shoot her a smile.

"You're coming tomorrow, right?"

"I wouldn't miss it. Although Salverton is a hike and a half."

"You could ride the spirit bus. It leaves from school in the morning."

Lily barks out a laugh. "Right—I'm just full of school spirit. I think I'd rather drive."

"All right. Well, thanks." I lean over and give her a hug. "We may not have traveling pants, but you're as good as any sister I could ever have."

Lily shakes her head, smiling. "Come on, Hallmark. Save the waterworks for Prince Charming out there."

I nod, but I don't say anything. Honestly, I think I've already cried all the tears I had left for Tommy Lawson.

I wait for Lily to pull away from the house before taking a deep breath and turning to face him. He's sitting on the front stoop, a bouquet of red roses in one hand. I can't help but think of the Monday after the county meet, when he showed up with the same bouquet and the same sweet smile. At the time, I'd been so sure of his love, even though he hadn't said it. Now I know better.

Roses are just roses.

Smiles are just smiles.

There isn't a double meaning or hidden agenda behind something as simple as a flower or a facial expression.

"Hey," he says, standing up to greet me. I stop walking and stand about five feet away from him.

"Hey," I say slowly. He reaches across the space to hand me the flowers, but I shake my head. "What are you doing here, Tommy?"

He sets the bouquet on the cement step and shoves his hands in his pockets.

"You weren't answering my calls. You ignored all my texts. I told you in the last one, if I had to stand in your driveway to get you to talk to me, that's what I'd do."

"I've already said everything I have to say to you."

"That's not true—you didn't say *anything* to me. You wrote it."

"Same difference." Blinking, I look up at him. He's shaking his head, a fierce expression on his face.

"What do you want me to say?" I ask, unable to keep the sarcasm from leaking into my voice. Tommy sighs.

"I don't know, Marijke. I just don't believe that after so much time together, you're really ready to throw it all away because of one night."

I stare at him for a second. His hair is messy and tousled in that sexy way I love. His eyes are darker than usual, and they lack their normal glint of good humor. I wonder if he's hurting the way I am. I wonder if he knows how hard it's been for me to let him go.

"My parents are separating."

Tommy's eyes widen, but he doesn't say anything, so I continue.

"That's why I wanted you to come over on Monday. They told me when I got home from practice. That's why I texted you and told you it was important."

"Jeez, baby," he says, shoving a hand back through his hair and messing it up even more. "I had no idea—I wish I'd known. Are you okay?"

I shrug. "My dad's staying at a hotel near his work. Mom seems sad a lot of the time, but we haven't really talked about it that much."

"Did they tell you why? Like, did one of them meet someone or something?"

"I don't think so. Mom just said that they got married when they were really young and they feel like they've held each other back."

I scuff my shoe against the brick border around the flowerbed.

"I feel terrible that I didn't even notice they were having problems. I guess I was just too wrapped up in us to care about anything else."

Before I can stop him, Tommy moves forward and pulls me toward him. I can't help myself. His arms feel good around me and his chest feels solid and strong. I've missed him so much over the past few days. All I needed was for him to hold me like this. I feel his lips press against my forehead.

"Baby, I'm so sorry. Truly. I-I had no clue that was going on. I swear to you, I would have been here in a heartbeat."

His lips begin to travel, pressing against my temple, then my cheek, then my jaw, and finally the corner of my mouth. I suck in a breath and he takes it as an invitation.

"I missed you so much," he murmurs against my lips before pulling me closer and deepening the kiss. For a second, I let myself go, losing all of my thoughts and new convictions in the power of that kiss.

And then I remember how I felt waking up Tuesday morning, knowing he'd never even bothered to come by. And I remember how I felt when he stood me up to go play paintball with his buddies. And I remember how I felt when I saw the texts and Facebook messages from other girls.

I jerk back, covering my mouth with one hand. My whole body is shaking. Tommy reaches for me again, but I stumble even farther backwards.

"I can't do this."

"Marijke," Tommy says, his voice uncharacteristically frantic, "come on. You know we belong together. You know this is right."

I shake my head. "No, this *isn't* right, Tommy. You have no idea what I've been putting myself through for the past month. For longer than that, really. You probably didn't even notice how miserable I've been."

Tommy swallows hard. "Okay. I-I guess I just thought you were being jealous."

"Maybe I *was* being jealous. But that's not why this is over. It's over because I've been *living my life* for you, I've let everything revolve around you. I didn't get my driver's license. I haven't even picked a college because I was waiting to see what you decided to do next year. I built my world around you!"

His expression changes a bit as I yell at him. This time he looks a little frustrated.

"I never asked you to do that."

"I know that."

"So then, why did you?"

"Because I love you!"

Suddenly, it's like the world stops. I don't hear any birds chirping or cars driving by. The wind ceases to blow. It's just me and Tommy, staring at each other. Is it just my imagination, or has my boyfriend—my *ex*-boyfriend—turned pale at the three words I've held back from saying for so long?

"If you love me," he says slowly, "then why are you breaking up with me? That doesn't make any sense."

"I know. It doesn't, but this relationship feels totally one-sided. Love has to be a partnership. It doesn't matter how much I love you if you don't love me back."

"Who says I don't love you?"

I stare at him, one brow cocked. "Sometimes it's about what you *don't* say, not what you do."

Tommy groans. "You know how I feel about you."

Shaking my head, I move around him and start walking toward the front door of the house.

"No, I don't know how you feel. And that's the point. I don't need flowers or gifts or songs you wrote or anything like that. I just need you to *tell me* how you really feel. And you can't give me that, can you?"

I give him a five-second window to respond. He looks at me, his expression half-cautious and half-confused, as if he doesn't know what I'm asking for.

I look at him sadly. "It's over, Tommy. I'm sorry. I can't do this anymore."

"Wait—please—I just—"

I hold a hand up. "Just go."

He's still talking when I turn to unlock the door. He's practically pleading when I open it, but I block out his words. It doesn't matter what he says now.

"Baby, please" are the last words I hear as I shut the door firmly in his face. I don't wait for a knock or the sound of the doorbell. Instead, I hurry toward the kitchen and away from the temptation to let him inside.

And that's when I see the stack of college materials, sitting at a precarious tilt on the side table, with North Carolina State's insignia printed boldly on the very top envelope.

I hear General Qi's distinctive engine roar to life just as I drop into a chair at the kitchen table. As Tommy drives away, I pull out the NCU acceptance letter and close my eyes. It's time to make a decision without any outside factors. It's time to make a choice.

And I choose me.

FORTY

⇒ LILY ⇐

"Mom, I'm heading to the track meet!"

I wait for her response, but she doesn't say anything. I move closer to the stairs and try again.

"Mom?"

"Wait, Lily. Hold on for a second."

I can hear her talking, her voice rushed and a little sharp. I wonder if she's being stood up again. Maybe she's having a fight with Jim.

"I'm coming with you."

I look up at her, startled. This is the last thing I expected to hear from my mother. But she's pulled on an old Molesworth High hoodie from her days as a student and she's bounding down the stairs.

"Since Mac's with his dad for the weekend and since you and I have never gone to a Molesworth sporting event, I figure we should give it a shot."

"I—okay . . . if you really want to."

She nods emphatically. "I *really* want to."

Mom insists on driving, so I settle in the passenger seat of her Cherokee and resist the urge to turn on my iPod and get lost in my music. The last thing I feel like doing is chatting with my mom during the hour-long car ride to Salverton.

"So why'd you decide to come with me?" I ask her as she backs out of the driveway.

"Because I broke up with Jim."

I turn to stare at her. "Seriously?"

She gives me a sad little smile.

"Yep. Seriously."

"Why?"

Mom sighs and runs a hand through her hair.

"I guess I just decided that I shouldn't be with someone who doesn't really want to be with me."

I shake my head. "Wow. Well, I never thought I'd see the day."

Mom goes quiet for a second, then clears her throat.

"You know, it really hurts me when you say stuff like that."

I look at her incredulously. "Are you kidding?"

"No."

I close my eyes, attempting to restrain the emotion I feel bubbling up to the surface. But I can't—and like a science-project volcano, it froths and spills over with abandon.

"Do you have any idea how many times—for how many *years*—you've been hurting *me*?"

Mom glances over at me, eyes a little watery. I'm not having any of it.

"You have spent my entire life trying to find a man. You've sacrificed time that belonged to Mac and to me. Time that we should have spent with you, you were spending with guys like Contractor Jim."

"Lily, honey . . ."

"No." I shake my head vigorously, refusing to meet her gaze. "You made me believe that I wasn't as important to you as your love life."

My eyes are dry, but the tears are gathering around the lump in my throat. I try to swallow them back. Mom, on the other hand, is openly weeping. I can hear the sniffles, but still I won't look at her.

"I'm sorry, sweetie," she says finally.

I pretend to ignore her and she grows quiet. For the next twenty minutes, the only thing I can hear is the faint melody of music over the radio and the rumble of the tires meeting the road.

It isn't until we get to the Salverton city limits that she decides to speak again. This time, though, she surprises me.

"You're right."

I look over at her, eyes narrowed. "About what?"

"About what you said. About who I was and what I did. I

did put you and Mac on the back burner. I *did* make selfish decisions all in the name of love. I was desperate to feel that feeling, Lily. That movielike happily ever after that so many people have. I wanted that too. I *still* want it."

She takes a deep breath and tries to steady her voice.

"But I made bad choices. I know I can be a great mom, but I should have made sure you and Mac know that, no matter what, you're my first priority. I'm sorry I didn't do that."

I look at her then. In her own way, my mom looks a lot like me: dark hair with untamable curls, bright eyes that focus on the details of every plan, and a strong, independent streak. I haven't seen that independence in her for a long time. Now, though, it's kind of like it never disappeared at all.

I reach out and pat her hand.

"Let's just have a fun day together, Mom. It's a good place to start."

By the time we make it to the track, we're almost thirty minutes late, so we take a seat on the bleachers just in time to watch the four-person relay race ending. I can see Marijke down at the sidelines, chatting with Beth Stuart, while Coach Mason paces back and forth. He looks a little nervous. In fact, so does Marijke.

I glance over along the bleachers and see Tommy sitting all the way at the opposite end. By the direction he's staring,

I know he's watching Marijke. He looks miserable; his frown and the dark circles under his eyes aren't hard to see, even from this distance.

As I scan the crowd on the lower bleachers, I see a familiar dark head with tousled hair. I suck in a breath. At least his back is to me. With any luck, Joe won't realize that I'm sitting behind him. The best-case scenario will be Molesworth wins and I slip out unnoticed.

A voice comes over the loudspeaker, announcing the hurdling event, and I watch Marijke shake the hand of one of her opponents, then fold into a runner's starting position. When the shotgun sounds, I'm out of my seat without even realizing it. Immediately, half of the spectators on the bleachers do the same thing. We all watch Marijke and her opponents fly down the track toward the first hurdle. As each of them leap over the white obstacles, I realize I'm holding my breath in anticipation.

For a second, time stands still. Or maybe it leaps forward. Regardless, I watch Marijke fly over each hurdle as if it's nothing at all, and I can imagine the fierce determination on her face. In that moment, I'm so proud of her. She's running toward her future with every step she takes.

From this distance, it's hard to tell who wins. There's an overall sense of confusion as Marijke and the other runners come to a stop. Coach Mason is sprinting toward her, along with Beth and a few other girls. It isn't until they hoist

Marijke on their shoulders that I realize Molesworth High girls' track has won the state championship. As everyone else realizes the same thing, there is a rising roar that overtakes the crowd. Soon the fans on the bleachers are storming the field and track. Everyone is running toward the center and I see streamers fly through the air. Someone repeatedly blows an air horn. There's mass chaos, but it's a happy kind of disorder.

I grin at my mom and point at the track. "I'm gonna run down there and congratulate her before we go, okay?"

"Sure—I'll go say hello to Coach Mason. I wonder if he'll remember me from back in the day."

I bound down the middle of the bleachers as if they're stairs and hop down into the grass. From here, I see Marijke is still elevated on someone's shoulders and being spun in circles. I push through the crowd; when I finally reach her and she sees me, she makes the girls put her down on the ground.

"Wow," she says, stumbling a little. "I'm a little wobbly now. Maybe I need to be carried around all day."

I grin and reach in to hug her. "Congratulations. You rocked it."

"I think all the practice paid off in the end." She beams at me.

"You look really happy," I tell her. She shrugs.

"I am, I think. I'm definitely happy about that race!"

Which is when a male voice calls her name. We both turn to see Tommy, his hands in his pockets, standing a few yards away.

"Should I tell him to get lost?" I ask under my breath. But she shakes her head.

"No, it's fine. I'll catch up with you later, all right?"

"Sure."

I look at Tommy briefly. He looks almost as depressed as before, save the sad little glimmer of hope in his eye when he looks at Marijke.

I move back toward the bleachers, weaving in and out of the people around me. But I'm not paying close enough attention to where I'm walking and, as if by some kind of divine manifestation, I run right into a tall male body.

"Oof!"

I grunt, attempting steady myself by inadvertently grabbing the stranger's shoulders. But, of course, he's not a stranger. His green eyes flash with surprise and then a touch of amusement.

"We've got to stop meeting this way, Lily Spencer," Joe says in his gravely voice.

He's smiling now and I just stare up at him, speechless. *Damn it!*

How does he render me so completely paralyzed? How is it possible I'm unable to flee him, despite my desire to run away?

FORTY-ONE

⇒ MARIJKE ⇐

There's good reason that romantic comedies are so successful: They are predictable. They are perfect. They have a script to follow and a formula that creates the perfect chemistry and connection every time. That's what Lily and I forgot when we put together our master plan. Life isn't predictable like a movie. There isn't a formula to follow.

"Hey," I finally say to Tommy, at a loss for what should come after that. He takes a step forward.

"Um, congratulations. State champion—I bet it feels good after you've worked so hard."

I nod, watching him. His eyes look tired and sad, so unlike the eyes I've known for more than a year. He's usually so full of life, but standing here he's like a muted version of his bright self.

"What are you doing here, Tommy?"

He shrugs. "I, uh—I just wanted to be here. To support you. I wasn't even going to tell you that I came. I was hoping to just come and go without you seeing me. But, well, I couldn't resist telling you how proud I am of you."

I give him a sad smile and run a hand over my ponytail.

"Well, thanks. I think I'm glad you came."

It's an honest response and he deserves that, since he's being so honest with me.

"Me too." He rocks back on his heels and looks around us at the still-celebrating crowd. "Is everyone going for pizza?"

"Yeah—we called ahead this time, though. I think we'll have at least double the turnout. Salvatore might have a heart attack."

"Do you mind if I come along?"

I cock my head, taking a deep breath.

"I don't know—I really just want to spend some time with the team. It's our last big hurrah, you know?"

"Yeah, okay." He looks up at the sky, then back at me. "What about tonight? Maybe I could come over later? We could talk . . ."

"I'm hanging with my mom tonight. I promised her we'd spend some time together."

Tommy nods, and I can't help but feel a little bad.

"I'm not trying to avoid you. Maybe you can come by later."

He gives me a sad smile. "No, I get it. You have a life

and it doesn't revolve around me. I'm sorry I made you feel like it had to for so long. I'm sorry I ever made you question how important you are to me."

"Tommy . . . ," I say warily. "I really can't do this right now."

"Right." He scrubs a hand over his face. "Listen, I just came here to show you support. And I wanted to ask you— I mean, if you'd be willing, I'd like to take you out next week. On a date."

I heave another sigh. Next week is prom. *That's* the date we should be going on.

"I don't know," I finally say.

"Okay, well, think about it. I've planned something that I think you'll really like."

I nod because I'm not sure what else to do.

"Thanks for coming," I say again. My voice is a little weak. He shrugs.

"No problem. I'll . . . I'll see you around, I guess."

"Yeah. See you around."

As he walks away, I exhale the breath I didn't realize I'd been holding. Somehow, this isn't exactly the confrontation I'd been playing out in my mind. It wasn't the groveling I thought I wanted. He hadn't begged and cried and confessed his love. And I strangely find myself feeling glad about it. I don't know what I would have done if he said he loved me now.

Maybe I would have said that I love me too.

FORTY-TWO

⟩ LILY ⟨

"I was hoping you'd be here," Joe says, reaching out to grab my hand. "I missed you at the charity race last night."

I swallow hard.

"I, uh, I gotta go meet my mom . . ."

I attempt to release my hand, but he laces his fingers with mine and starts walking to the other side of the bleachers.

"Where are we going?" I snap at him. "I told you, I have to go."

"No."

"No?" I stare at him and he shakes his head, his expression solemn.

"No. We need to talk."

He drops my hand now and I sigh.

"Joe, I've already made enough of a fool of myself. I'd really like to go now."

He moves forward, faster than I would have thought possible, and blocks me from walking back.

"I've been thinking about that day in my truck."

"Please don't do this." The shell around my heart starts to thicken. I refuse to let him hurt me again.

"I want to take you out. Like, on a date."

I blink up at him, dumbstruck. Despite my efforts against it, I can feel fissures start to spread in the protective casing around my heart.

"I asked you if you wanted to go out, and you said no," I argue. "You said you didn't want something serious."

I can hear my breath quicken as Joe reaches out to cup my chin.

"I also told Barbara I couldn't go to the prom with her."

"But . . . why?"

His lips curl into a sexy smile I can only describe as swoonworthy.

"Because I want to go with *you*. Because I can't wait to dance at our senior prom with *you*."

I stare at him, dumbfounded. I don't even know how to react, but the elation coursing through me proves my body knows exactly how to take this news.

"So that's what I wanted to say," he says, his voice husky. His hand is still on my face, stroking my cheek. "Tell me I'm not too late. Tell me we can go the prom together. Say yes."

"I-I don't know," I finally say, my eyes staring up into his with uncertainty.

Joe moves his hand back into my hair and pulls me a little closer. "Please, Lily. Take a chance on me."

I think about everything that's happened—about the missed opportunities and the crossed wires. About the failed attempts at movie magic and the times when I was so sure the movies would do the trick. And here we are, practically *under* the bleachers—the most nondescript, least romantic setting ever—and Joe Lombardi is asking me to our senior prom.

"I want to say yes," I admit. "I just don't know if I should."

"You should," he says confidently.

"Well, obviously you think that," I say, rolling my eyes. "But I—"

And then he leans in and plants his lips on mine.

When Joe kisses me, I can't help but think about science. About how experiments often cause variables that were unforeseen and about how no one can predict unpredictable reactions. There are times when the way you plan the procedure just isn't how the experiment works itself out. Instead, there's almost always an alteration to the plan. A step that you missed when you were writing out the to-do list.

A wild card.

Joe's lips are warm and soft, navigating mine carefully and with some skill. One of his hands moves into my hair and the other pulls my body even closer to his. I can feel his inherent warmth and I can smell the sun on his skin.

When we finally break apart, we're both smiling and breathless.

"Who knew an afternoon in detention would lead to this?" he whispers, his face still close to mine.

I smile at him and shake my head.

"I think it actually started in the stairwell."

FORTY-THREE

⇒ MARIJKE ⇐

It's just getting dark by the time Beth drops me off at my house. I'm so full of deep-dish pizza that I practically roll out of her car. The light is on in the living room and I wonder if Mom is just sitting there, waiting for me to get home.

For the first time in the history of ever, my parents came to my meet and sat separately. I haven't told a lot of people about their split, but seeing them sitting so far apart probably clued them in. Mom didn't come for pizza because Dad really wanted to since I wouldn't see him until next weekend. Once things had settled down at Salvatore's, Dad told me he was officially filing for a separation next week.

"I'm sorry, honey," he'd said softly. I'd shrugged. What other response was there? Even my parents and their picture-perfect marriage hadn't survived. I can't believe I ever thought my high school romance would make it in the end.

"Hey Mom," I call when I make it inside.

"Hey sweetie." She comes into the foyer and slides the strap of my track duffel from my shoulder. "You must be beat. You ready to veg out and watch a movie?"

"Sure."

"Can you do me a favor first?" she asks, walking back toward the living room. "I think I left the cover off the grill out back. Can you go put it back on?"

"Uh, okay." I move toward the sliding-glass door at the far end of the kitchen. "Want me to grab some popcorn when I come back in?"

"Sounds good."

I don't know why I'm not suspicious about the curtains being drawn over the glass doors. It's not something Mom ever does, but it doesn't even occur to me to be cautious. So I throw them aside and reach for the handle. I've already pulled the door halfway open when I finally look up and notice the candles.

There are hundreds of them. Big candles. Small candles. Candles lining the walkway. Candles floating in the pool.

And a cake covered in candles sitting on the patio table, where Tommy is standing, wearing a tuxedo.

I suck in a breath. This is the last thing I expected. Of all the movies I watched, of all the plans I'd made, *I* was always the one acting out the crazy scenes. It was never Tommy pulling a page or two from the Hollywood playbook.

"Tommy."

It's all I can manage to say. He holds up a hand.

"Please—just let me say this."

Then he moves so quickly toward me that I hardly have time to blink before he's taken my hands in his.

"You've spent endless hours trying to show me how much you love me. In your letter, you told me about all the planned dates, the choreographed dances, and you did all that stuff just for me. You wanted me to feel love. And I did feel your love, Marijke. I was just scared of it.

"The other night I watched that movie *Sixteen Candles*. When that Jake guy covers a cake with them to celebrate the redhead's birthday, something sort of clicked. I could see what you liked about the guys in those romantic comedies. They are willing to put themselves out there. They will say what's really in their hearts."

Tommy takes a deep breath and looks into my eyes. My heart seizes, then stutters.

"I should have told you this every day," he's saying, gripping my hands a little tighter, "and I'm so sorry I waited this long."

He pauses, then swallows.

"I love you, Marijke. I'm *in* love with you. I've never said that to anyone—I've never *felt* this way about anyone. But I know this is real. I can't imagine my life without you, and I'm begging you to give me another chance."

I almost choke on my own breathing. I stopped believing that Tommy was capable of this kind of gesture. Now that he's done it—well, I don't know if I want it anymore. Not if he's just trying to win me back for the sake of winning. I blink hard, the tears glossing over my eyes. As they begin to spill onto my cheeks, Tommy reaches up and brushes them away with one hand.

"Say something, baby," he says softly.

"What do you want me to say?" I ask. I hardly recognize my own voice.

"That you still love me. That I haven't screwed up too badly. That it's not too late."

"Too late for what? What are you asking for, Tommy?"

"For you. For you to be a strong and successful runner. For you to go to the college of your dreams or train for the Olympics or climb Mount Everest or do whatever you want to do. I believe in you. I want to be here for you. Let me prove it."

He steps back and reaches over to the cake. He slides it closer to the edge of the table and gestures for me to step closer.

"Read it. Please."

The wax from the birthday candles has started to pool around their bases, but I can still read the words scrawled in red icing.

WILL YOU GO TO PROM WITH ME?

"I asked you to go on one date with me next week," Tommy says. "And I know that prom is a big date, but I want it to be our first date—our *second* first date. I want to

walk into that room with you on my arm and everyone looking at us with all kinds of envy because we're so happy to be
together."

I swallow hard. He must know I'm still unsure, because
he puts a hand on my hip and I let him pull me into him
until our bodies are so close, I can feel the heat of his skin
and I can smell his aftershave. I can't help myself—I've
missed that smell so much, so I take a deep breath in.

"You know what else happens in movies, Marijke?" he
asks me, his voice soft. He reaches up and brushes a strand
of hair away from my eyes.

"What?"

"Second chances. The main characters make mistakes,
but they all realize it at the end and come back to fix what
they've done. I'm ready to fix my mistakes. It's just up to you
to let me."

"You aren't the only one who made mistakes," I say quietly. "I based my life around you. If that's the person you
want, Tommy, then you are out of luck. I'm not that girl
anymore."

"I'm counting on that."

I let my lips slide up into a smile. "Okay."

"Okay?" Tommy blinks rapidly. "Okay what?"

"Okay, I'll go to prom with you."

His grin shines brighter than the candles around us.
"So would it be okay if I kissed you? Just to seal the deal?"

I don't answer him. Instead, I rock up onto my tiptoes and press my lips against his first.

The sizzle is immediate. Tommy's lips against mine have always ignited something deep inside me. And there it is—the last aspect of the perfect movie romance: chemistry. It's the one thing that the movies capture that real life has in common. It's the one thing you can't fake, because it's as certain as science.

FORTY-FOUR

⇒ LILY ⇐

I always thought that when I went to my senior prom, it would be like one of those movies where the dance is held in some kind of fancy space. A ballroom or something. There'd be a punch bowl, of course. I mean, what prom would be complete without a spikable punch bowl? The girls would be glamorous and the boys would be dapper. Inexplicably, that school would be able to afford a semifamous band to come play.

But this prom? Well, it's a little more rooted in reality. There's a DJ—the same lame DJ we had for homecoming. We're in the gym, where they hold all the dances, pretending that crepe paper and dimmed lights hide the basketball hoops. And the punch has been ditched in favor of bottled water, since the school board banned sugary drink distribution last fall.

But the way my date is looking at me right now, the way his arms are wrapped around me as we sway to the music— well, it makes any movie prom pale in comparison with my reality.

"Have I told you that you look amazing tonight?" Joe whispers close to my ear. I smile up at him.

"Yeah. A couple dozen times, I think."

"Good." His lips spread into a smile. "I don't want you to forget it."

"Hey Joe!" A junior guy—I think his name is Ben— punches Joe on the arm as he passes with his date. "Hey Lily."

"Lily, I adore your dress! It's totally amazing," his date sort of squeals. I have absolutely no idea who she is.

"Uh, thanks," I say, looking down at the beading on my black, spaghetti-strap gown. Joe sort of smirks at me.

"See—I told you so. You're beautiful."

I scoff. "Please. She was talking about my dress, not me."

Before he can argue, Courtney taps my shoulder.

"Hey Lily. Can you check on the junior volunteers? I think they should go ahead and replenish some of the refreshments. I've got to go get ready for the coronation."

I guess it doesn't surprise me that the SGA president is also nominated for prom queen. Still, I really hope Marijke wins it.

"Sure." I pull back from Joe, and Courtney grins at me, then him.

"Have a great night, guys."

Joe curls a hand around mine as we weave across the dance floor toward the back of the gym. Every few feet someone stops to say hello to one of us or to compliment me on my dress.

"Well, aren't you Little Miss Popular." Joe grins at me.

I can't help but laugh. The meaning of irony has never been so obvious as it is right now.

"I'm going to go find Marijke. I want to wish her luck."

"Okay, I'll take care of the food. Want me to beat the juniors into submission if the chips are too low?"

I laugh again.

"How about you just have them refill the bowls?"

"You take away all my fun," he says, pouting a bit in the most adorable way. Then suddenly he's pulled me close.

"Hurry back, okay," he murmurs. When he leans in and kisses me, it feels like a promise. I've never felt so much potential in my life.

"I will," I say breathlessly once he releases me. He winks and turns me around, steering me toward the stage.

It takes a few minutes to locate Marijke, but when I do, I'm struck by how happy she looks. She's practically glowing in her ice-blue dress and silver strappy heels. Tommy is standing next to her, holding her hand and whispering something in her ear.

When she sees me approaching, she grins and runs forward to hug me.

"You look great, Lil," she says, pulling back to look me over. "At least some of that makeover managed to seep into your psyche."

I laugh. "Don't let it go to your head. Are you nervous?"

Marijke shrugs one shoulder and waves a hand. "Nah. Piece of cake."

Then she looks me in the eye and I know she's lying. And she *knows* I know she's lying. That's the kind of friends we've become. The kind who can read each other with just a look.

"Good luck," I say, hugging her once again as she heads toward the stage steps. I smile at Tommy before walking back to find Joe.

When the crowds part, I live a moment eerily similar to the scene in *Sixteen Candles*—the one where Samantha is outside the church and the cars drive away in both directions, leaving Jake and his red race car in full view. Joe is leaning against the wall, and he watches me as I approach.

"Come here," he says.

I move into his arms as the amp buzzes to life behind me. Principal Campen clears his throat and taps the microphone.

"Ladies and gentlemen, it's the moment you've all been waiting for."

The crowd gets quiet as he unfolds a paper in his hands.

"This year's prom king and queen are . . . Tommy Lawson and Marijke Monti!"

I can see from a distance as Marijke bounds up the stairs, then turns and runs back down them straight into Tommy's arms. He lifts her up and spins her around while everyone laughs. Then they hurry back up the stairs together. Marijke grins at Mr. Campen, and Tommy takes a sweeping bow. The audience cheers, and I clap right along with them.

"You know," Joe says in my ear, "if I were in charge, I would have made you prom queen."

I smile up at him. "Nah. That's Marijke's happily ever after, not mine."

"So then, what's your happily ever after?"

The music begins again, a slow, low melody, and I see Tommy leading Marijke out to the middle of the dance floor. Other couples are joining them, so I tug Joe's hand and we move closer to the center. Once we're surrounded by dancers, I turn and wrap my arms around his neck. He settles his hands at my waist and pulls me close.

"You didn't answer my question," he reminds me.

I take a deep breath, then lean into his chest. I let the scent of his cologne and the lights of the DJ booth and the flutter of the streamers combine into a ball of something that could only be considered cinematic.

"So what's your happily ever after, Lily?" he repeats.

If this were a movie, cameras would be zooming in on me right now. I lean back again and smile up at Joe.

"This."

⇒ ACKNOWLEDGMENTS ⇐

No writer is an island. I have so many people to thank:

First, to the filmmakers, actors, and production staff who made all the movies mentioned in the book possible. This book literally would not exist without the genius that is the romantic comedy. I'm indebted.

My agent, Suzie Townsend, is the best—her support, savvy, and talent are all qualities I've benefited from and continue to admire. Likewise, my editor, Mary Kate Castellani, gave this book room to grow and manifest into something special. She is the best possible person for me to work with. I'm one lucky writer.

Hannah Brown Gordon and everyone at Foundry Literary + Media, Joanna Volpe and everyone at New Leaf Literary, Bridget Hartzler and everyone at Bloomsbury Children's Books—I am so incredibly fortunate to have so many people in my corner.

In high school, Marijke Morris was one of the nicest, loveliest, happiest girls I knew. When I started writing this book, I thought a lot about Marijke—and, with her mother's blessing, decided to use her name for my main character. The world lost Marijke far too soon. I owe a debt of thanks to Frannie Sherwood and the rest of Marijke's family—especially her two beautiful little girls. She has left behind a beautiful legacy.

My family has earned a huge thank-you, especially Mom, Dad, Ryan, Kitty, Cassie, Kristy, Laura, and Danny. A special thank-you to my son, Max, who is my greatest inspiration.

Suzanne Klinejohn-Jones and Heather Templeton are former colleagues and friends who have been invested in this journey with me since very early on. Thanks for your support, ladies. You gave me someone to talk to and share good news with, and I love you for that.

I don't have biological sisters, but I'm fortunate enough to have these girls: Katie, who might still own every Disney movie on VHS; Lauren, who watched *Heathers* with me more times than I can count; Carly, who cried with me in the theater when we saw the *Sex and the City* movie; and Trisha, who can probably still recite every line from *Love & Basketball*. I owe each of you a dozen sleepovers, a thousand cupcakes, and all my love.

And for Josh—thank you for loving me enough to get behind this crazy writing life. I never knew how happy I could really be until now.

Kelly Fiore has a BA in English from Salisbury University and an MFA in poetry from West Virginia University. She has received two Individual Artist Awards from the Maryland State Arts Council. She is the author of *Taste Test*, *Just Like the Movies*, and *Thicker Than Water*. Kelly lives in West Virginia with one husband, three kids, two dogs, a cat, and a hedgehog.

www.kellyfiorewrites.com
@kellyannfiore

WANT MORE OF WHAT YOU CAN'T HAVE?

if only

Kristin Rae

WHAT YOU ALWAYS WANTED

AVAILABLE MARCH 2016

BLOOMSBURY

*Read on for a glimpse at another **If Only** romance*
about a girl on a search for her dream guy, who
might just happen to live next door . . .

Contrary to popular belief, Texas is not all tumbleweeds, cacti, and horses. I haven't seen a desert yet, and the people in Houston mostly look the same as people from back home, but with the occasional set of cowboy boots. And the restaurants we've tried so far aren't too bad, though they cook everything in butter. Then cover it with gravy.

Apparently there's zero public transportation in my new north-side community except for some little trolley thing to take you between the mall, the grocery store, and the library. But it's more cute than useful, especially since I live down a dirt road even farther north from everything. People here seem to favor driving their own pickup trucks. I can probably count on one hand the number of times I've ridden in a truck, but now feel like I must have one too. Or at least something with four wheels. And soon.

We've lived here exactly six days. School starts in three. School as in my new school. As in I get to start all over for my junior year, minus everyone I know. Minus every*thing* I know.

And it's hot here. The melt-your-face-off kind of hot. Our mailbox is way out at the street next to the driveway, not up by the door like I'm used to. So here I am in my new Southern life, forced to walk the acre-long driveway in the scorching August sun because the really good classic movies are only available to rent on disc. I shake my fist in the air at the hypothetical Netflix gods before opening the rusted contraption.

Perfect. Mail's not even here yet. I wouldn't mind so much if I didn't feel like I had to take a shower every time I came in from outside. I smell like a wet dog that just rolled in grass clippings.

I turn to head back to the house and hear gravel crunch under tires as a vehicle pulls out of the driveway across the street. It doesn't drive off, so I toss a curious glance at the cherry-red Tahoe. The window glides down, revealing a woman around my parents' age with highlighted hair in a wedge cut and a chunky turquoise necklace that might possibly be choking her.

"How's the move-in going?" she calls out to me.

I shrug and relax my eyes as a cloud passes over. If I told her the whole truth, I'd sound like a huge whiner. "We'll be living out of boxes for a while. The house needs to be fixed up. A *lot*." I take a few steps closer as she cuts off the engine.

She nods and gives a little snicker. "Yeah, the last people that lived there were a little . . . grubby. I'm Sherri Morales," she says. "Where did y'all move from?"

"Maddie Brooks. We're from Chicago."

"Really? I'm from Michigan. Well, haven't lived there in twenty years, but I grew up there." She glances at her fancy silver watch. "Are you starting school on Monday?"

"Yes," I say through a frown. "I'll be a junior."

"Aw, why the sour face? I'm sure you'll be just fine. My daughter Angela is a sophomore, but she'd love to show you the ropes. And I'll be there too since I'm the theatre teacher. I also help run the Fernwood Community Playhouse in town."

My jaw drops. "You're kidding me. You're the theatre teacher? I'm signed up for your class, then!" I rush to her and grip the door at the window opening, putting us face-to-face. "What productions are we doing this year? Can you give me a heads-up?"

She doesn't look shocked by my burst of enthusiasm. "Oh, I'm still finalizing the calendar. Got the acting bug, do you?"

"More like a disease."

She smiles, eyes wide. "Well, show me what you've got."

Without missing a beat, I look her dead in the eye and recite one of my favorite bits from *Barefoot in the Park*.

I inwardly celebrate my delivery. I'd worked on memorizing the script last spring for an audition I missed because of the move. At least I'm getting some use out of it.

Mrs. Morales cocks her head to the side and surprises me with the next line of dialogue.

Boosted with confidence, I say what's next and we go back and forth in an impromptu performance in the middle of the street until she says, "If you always perform that well, you'll have no problem keeping up with my core team."

"Thank you!" I resist the urge to jump up and down.

She gazes out the windshield. "I haven't thought about that play in a really long time. Most kids your age haven't even heard of it—the play or the movie."

"Oh, I adore the movie," I sigh, placing a hand over my heart. "Robert Redford. So hot."

"Are you sure you're in high school?" Mrs. Morales rests her head against the seatback and laughs. "Well, I can't tell you how refreshing this conversation is, Maddie Brooks." She checks her watch again and reaches for the keys in the ignition. "You don't happen to have plans tonight, do you?"

Thinking she's about to ask me to accompany her to a play or to dinner so we can discuss my future on Broadway, I shake my head. "No friends here yet."

No friends anywhere.

"Would you mind watching my five-year-old, Elise, for a couple hours? Angela may not speak to me for a week if I make her stay home another Friday night."

I deflate. That's nowhere near as fun. I've always avoided babysitting like the dentist. Snotty noses, whining, all the questions. Makes me shudder.

"I'll give you fifty bucks."

On the other hand, babysitting can be quite lucrative. The little darling shall love me.

Around six o'clock, I start the marathon down their driveway. The house isn't visible from the road, so I have no idea what to expect—if it's small and rundown like my new house or . . . a freaking mansion.

The two-story, stucco house spreads wide across the clearing of tall pines and oak trees. Obviously, the Morales family has a lot more land than we do.

A robin's-egg blue Dodge truck that looks older than my parents' rests off to the side, next to a newer, bright yellow Beetle. I don't see Mrs. Morales's Tahoe anywhere.

I knock on the huge wooden door, and a few seconds later a girl near my age but a couple inches taller than me opens it. She looks exactly like her mother, but only in body frame and facial features—same green eyes and full lips. Her shoulder-length hair is almost black and she has that pretty olive skin tone that makes me jealous. The Latin last name is making more sense to me now.

"Maddie, right?" she asks.

"Angela, right?"

"Come on in," she says, turning and waddling back into the house, her shiny red toes separated with foam.

I follow her past a grand wooden staircase to the kitchen. She plops down at a round dining table and works on her fingernails. Her left hand looks pretty good but the right is sloppy with paint all over her skin.

"That looks terrible," I say.

She grunts and turns her head back the way we came. "Elise! Your sitter's here!"

There's stomping overhead and a little voice shouts, "I'm staying in my room!"

I spot two twenty-dollar bills on the counter by the phone. "Did your mom leave that for me?"

She nods, then yells, "Elise, get down here and meet her before I leave."

More thumping from upstairs. "No! I have chalk hands. Mom said I can't go downstairs with chalk hands."

Fantastic.

"Then wash them! Don't make me count!" Angela swipes at her pinky nail but the brush hits more of her skin than the actual nail. "Chalk hands," she mutters.

"And you have nail polish hands," I say, pocketing the twenties. I notice a ten-dollar bill under a set of keys on the kitchen island. Pretty sure that's supposed to be mine too.

Angela douses a cotton ball with remover and attacks her fingers. "I can't do this. I'll never get it."

"Whoa, whoa, you're going to mess up your good hand." I sit next to her and wet a new cotton ball. "Here, let me."

"Elise!" she calls again. "I swear, that girl. She's like a little kid or something."

We laugh as I carefully paint her nails. This feels so normal, like any other Friday night, my friends and I painting each other's trouble hands. But I've been here for two minutes. All I know about this girl is that she can yell really loudly and she thinks she's putting one over on me.

"So," I begin, "about that ten dollars over there. . . ."

She covers her mouth with her other hand and groans. "She told you how much she was giving you?"

"Uh, yeah." I blow on her fingertips out of habit, then stop myself because really, I wouldn't want a stranger blowing on my hand.

"I'm sorry." Her forehead falls to the table with a little thud. "She never gives me any money, not even when I watch Elise. But she'll pay *you* to do it." She snaps her head up to look at me. "No offense."

I shrug, wondering if Rider ever went through any of this with me when we were younger. Not that he's that much older than me—just a couple of years—but it must be a pain having to watch a sibling. So glad I don't have to deal with that.

"I didn't even have any real plans besides trying to get my friend Tiffany to go to the mall with me. There's this cute guy that works at the candy apple kiosk," Angela explains. "I mean, how lame is it to hang out on the weekend with a five-year-old? No offense there either."

"Hey, I have an excuse. I don't know anyone yet."

Once we moved, I sort of made this plan to be a mopey introvert. I was going to act so alone and depressed that my parents would have to send me back to Chicago and I'd find a way into my old social circle—they distanced themselves after my dad lost his job and moved us to Texas, so admittedly, not the most genuine group of girls. But that's not exactly a realistic scheme, and I really want to be accepted here. I'm too needy to give up friends entirely.

Angela inspects her nails before blowing on them. "Thanks. They look great." She sighs, leaning back in her chair.

"Well," I begin, "if you really don't have anything to do tonight, what if we split the money and watch Elise together?"

She hesitates and instantly I feel like an idiot. This girl is a grade below me. I'm guessing she's the one who drives the Beetle the color of sunshine that begs to be seen on the road, and I'm asking her to stay in on a Friday night. Look how desperate I am to make a friend. I'm bribing her with money that she already stole.

"I could paint your nails," she finally says.

I try to tone down my eagerness. "Sure!"

After she does a decent job turning my nails a shimmery pink, Angela leads me up the staircase to meet Elise. Her bedroom is a purple explosion of pillows and stuffed animals, with three lilac walls and one black with chalkboard paint covered in doodles. A girl in jean shorts and a blue shirt turns her back on her masterpiece to face us, three fat sticks of chalk in her hands. I'm surprised to find that her hair's nearly blond.

"Lookit!" Elise points to a drawing of a pink house among flowers the size of trees.

"It's beautiful!" Angela picks up a few stray pieces of chalk from the floor and puts all but one into a bucket near the wall. "You're a true artist, don't you think so, Maddie?"

Elise looks at me shyly out of the corner of her eye. I'm not used to little kids, so I'm not really sure how to interact with them. But I'm getting paid for this, so I might as well make an effort.

"I think you're fantastic," I begin. "Best flower-drawer I've ever seen!"

This wins her over. She smiles and shows me a huge patch of chalk flowers in the corner by her dresser, going up as high as she can reach. "They're my favorite! Big ole daisies."

Angela writes ELISE in yellow block letters in the blank space above the house.

"Hey, that's my name!" Elise giggles then turns to me. "What's your name look like?"

I make sure my nails are dry before taking the stick of chalk from Angela, and I spell out my name next to hers, drawing a little daisy as the dot over the *I*. Elise claps and I smile back at her, strangely pleased that I've just been approved by a five-year-old.

Angela wipes her hands on a towel hanging over the edge of the chalk bucket. "Maddie and I are going to play with you tonight, how does that sound?"

"Okay," Elise says, also wiping off her hands. "Can we have egg rolls? And white rice?"

"That sounds like a yummy idea," Angela says. "Go wash your hands and pick out a movie to watch, and I'll go order."

After we decide on sesame chicken to go with our egg rolls, Angela points me to the TV room at the end of the hall—a living area with a gigantic screen, a couple brown leather couches, and a built-in bookcase along the entire back wall. As long as I don't look up too high, I can ignore the deer heads mounted above the window. I wander to the bookcase to look at the collection of family photos, and learn there are a total of three children. Elise is the youngest, Angela's the middle child, and whoever *that* gorgeousness is had better be in my class come Monday. He's a little taller than Angela with spiky, near-black hair and the same green eyes. Man, these people make some pretty kids.

"That's Jesse," Angela says, startling me.

"Cool." If I were a blusher, I'd probably go tomato-faced. Nothing like getting caught drooling over a picture of someone's hot brother.

"Meh, he's pretty cool as far as brothers go, I guess." She plops down on the love seat and hollers, "Elise, come pick out a movie!"

"Is Jesse here somewhere? I'm guessing that's his blue truck in the driveway."

"It is, but he's out with friends. His popularity level is annoying."

Because I can't help myself, I glance at Jesse's image one more time before sitting on the other couch. "Popularity with girls, you mean?" As if that needed clarification.

"Everyone, but yes, girls especially." She wrinkles her nose in the sisterly way I know all too well.

"Don't worry," I say, feeling suddenly guilty for finding him attractive. I put my hand over my chest in hopes of making her laugh. "My heart belongs to another."

This seems to satisfy her, for now.

Anyway, I'm pretty sure no one's brother will ever be able to compare to the man of my dreams.

CHECK OUT ALL THE IF ONLY ROMANCES!

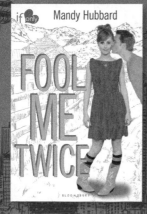

if only — Mandy Hubbard
FOOL ME TWICE

if only — Kristin Rae
WISH YOU WERE ITALIAN

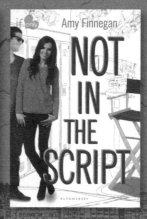

if only — Amy Finnegan
NOT IN THE SCRIPT

if only — Jessica Burkhart
WILD HEARTS

if only — Lauren Baratz-Logsted
RED GIRL, BLUE BOY

if only — Mandy Hubbard
EVERYTHING BUT THE TRUTH

if only — Kelly Fiore
JUST LIKE THE MOVIES

if only — Kristin Rae
WHAT YOU ALWAYS WANTED